THE CURE FOR REMEMBERING

THE CURE FOR REMEMBERING
A DR. NORA STERNBERG MYSTERY

RUTH E. WEISSBERGER, MD

MELVILLE HOUSE
PUBLISHING

HOBOKEN
NEW JERSEY

MELVILLE HOUSE PUBLISHING
300 OBSERVER HIGHWAY
THIRD FLOOR
HOBOKEN, NJ 07030

WWW.MHPBOOKS.COM

BOOK DESIGN: CAROL HAYES

ISBN: 978-1-933633-20-6

LIBRARY OF CONGRESS CATALOGING-IN-PUBLICATION DATA

WEISSBERGER, RUTH E.
  THE CURE FOR REMEMBERING : A DR. NORA STERNBERG MYSTERY /
RUTH E. WEISSBERGER.
   P. CM.
 ISBN 978-1-933633-20-6
 I. TITLE.
   PS3623.E459C87 2007
   813'.6--DC22

          2007027331

For my uncles, Ernie and Jack

CHAPTER ONE

Because of the flu, I had missed the conference in Banff on "molecular frontiers of hepatitis." I stayed in bed for three days, febrile and giddy with the television on, sleeping and waking at odd hours. My husband Brad called every day from Bergen, Norway, advising me to check myself into the hospital, which sounded quaint and almost Victorian, or, if I wouldn't do that, to go back to work. This reminded me of Dr. Garrett, the former chief of neurosurgery at Lafayette Medical Center, who was fond of observing that an intern should spend all his time in the hospital, either working or too sick to work. My friend and colleague Jessica Harvey also called periodically to see how I was doing and to cheer me up with ridiculous anecdotes from the latest medical staff meeting, which she was obliged to attend as President.

My other frequent caller, my great-aunt Selma, was a little miffed because I had told her not to visit me and expose herself to the flu. She didn't require instructions on when to visit the sick. She was a retired nurse extraordinaire, who for forty years had been a pillar of the Nursing Department at the hospital, long before it ever became the Medical Center where I had trained. Furthermore, she knew when to get a flu shot, unlike some doctors. In retrospect, if I hadn't been so presumptuous, everything might have turned out differently. Who knows? That's what I hate about retrospection.

As it was, I was stumbling around my apartment looking for Tylenol when an emergency room resident called me. Aunt Selma had fallen on the sidewalk outside her apartment building and fractured her hip. She had given my name as her emergency contact. I was touched because I knew Aunt Selma thought I was a zero in an emergency, unlike herself.

"Dr. Sternberg, what's your aunt's baseline mental status?" the resident asked.

This was an interesting question. "Normal," I answered; normal in a general sense. It was not the word that sprang to mind when describing a Sternberg.

"Then I don't know what's going on. She's completely oriented, but she's insisting on being transferred to another hospital, and she gets agitated when we tell her we don't think that's a good idea."

"Why does she want to be transferred?" I asked.

"I don't know," the resident said. "She wants to speak with you. Is it OK if I hand her the phone?"

"Of course," I said, baffled. Aunt Selma, as far as I had ever known, felt a great attachment and loyalty to the Medical Center. I figured she must have been delirious.

"Nora, I don't have much time," she whispered into the phone. "They're going to shoot me up with Thorazine or something."

"They don't use Thorazine that way any more, Aunt Selma," I said.

"It's not safe here. You have to get me out of here."

"Aunt Selma, do you know where you are?"

"Oh, here's Dr. Fabricant. Talk to him, Nora. Tell him to transfer me to another hospital." Before I could protest, I heard the phone being jostled and my aunt's worried voice asking her internist, Dr. Leon Fabricant, to speak with me.

"Hello, Nora," he drawled in his familiar, patronizing way. How Aunt Selma tolerated him was beyond me. "It seems your aunt fractured her femoral neck."

"What happened?"

"Well, we're not entirely sure," he said.

"I tripped on the curb," she rasped in the background. "You have to get me to another hospital!"

"Well, I think we have to rule out a syncopal episode," he continued.

"They can rule out syncope somewhere else!" she squeaked.

"Yes, well, you know, they say the worst patients in the world are doctors and nurses."

I snorted involuntarily at the telephone. "Tell Aunt Selma I'm coming right over," I said, and hung up.

Poor Aunt Selma, I thought. I knew she should have been on something for osteoporosis. She had smoked for a hundred years and had always been thin. But she never listened to my advice. In her prime she had been one of those commando nurses you sometimes still encounter in emergency departments. She had started as a scrub nurse in the operating room and had worked with some of the best surgeons of her generation, who were all men, of course. Talented as she was, she had learned, by watching and assisting, to do everything they did. So when the celebrated chest surgeon, Dr. James Atwells, had a seizure in the operating room in the middle of a thoracotomy, throwing the assisting surgeons and the anesthesiologist into a state of total confusion, it was Aunt Selma who stepped in and successfully completed the operation. That was in 1955. She never received any thanks or even acknowledgement from the hospital and, to my amazement, wasn't bitter. She never expected much, unlike the women doctors of my generation.

I careened from the living room to the bedroom and got myself dressed, stuffing a wad of tissues in my pocket. According to the weather reports, which I had watched numerous times in the past 72 hours, almost as many times as I had seen updates on the Gulf War, it was bitter cold throughout the New York metropolitan area. By contrast, I felt like a piece of meat roasting in the oven that was my overheated apartment. I grabbed my coat from the hall closet, checked to make sure my ID badge was in the pocket, and stepped into the dark hallway.

Outside, I floated like a hovercraft in a frosty vapor over West End Avenue one block crosstown and seven downtown to the hospital. When later reconstructing the events of that day, I realized it must have been about nine o'clock at night when I arrived at the emergency room. It was the winter of 1991, and the North Building, where the ER was located, had been under renovation for almost two years, eight months longer than originally projected. The entrance was a chaos of construction tunnels and scaffolding, so I used the main hospital entrance, deserted at that hour. I passed the ATM that had recently been installed in the lobby, threaded my way through the planters and trees in the atrium, and headed down the corridor to the Tower Building. After following a serpentine route, past the beginnings and ends of many other corridors, I reached the North Building and the inside entrance to the ER. Having done my internship and residency at the Medical Center, I knew my way around its sprawling buildings reflexively.

I fished the identification badge out of the clump of tissues in my pocket and swiped the metallic edge through the security box on the wall. The stiff door swung open with a deep electric buzz. Then I headed down the long hall past the x-ray suite and the patient elevators, toward the front of the "A" section. This area consisted of a vast, low-ceilinged, brightly-lit space with a U-shaped counter in the middle enclosing the nursing station and rows of cubicles around the perimeter, each demarcated from the other by a system of curtains. An enormous board on the front wall listed the patients' names, diagnoses, and locations, as if oblivious to the hospital's much-touted confidentiality policy. There I found, scrawled in red marker, *Sternberg, S., R. hip fx, 3*. And behind the curtain of cubicle 3 was Aunt Selma on a gurney and Leon Fabricant by her side. Aunt

Selma was leaning forward on the stretcher, hyperventilating, trying to get up.

"What are you doing, Aunt Selma?" I asked in alarm.

"Help me get up, Nora," she pleaded. "Don't let them keep me here. I'll die!" She had an intravenous line in her left arm and two of the chest leads from her EKG were dangling outside her hospital gown, resulting in a flat line on the monitor. A nurse walked by and announced to all of us, "I just gave her some morphine."

"You try to relax, dear," Fabricant oozed, tapping her shoulder and trying to push her back down on the stretcher. An orthopedic resident sprinted over and informed us, in that remarkably clean-cut, athletic manner of orthopedic residents, that she was being admitted to Dr. Carter's service and would be going up to her bed on 7-North momentarily.

"No, I won't," Aunt Selma snapped at him. "My niece is here now, and she's going to transfer me to Saint Stephen's Hospital."

We all gasped.

"Why would I do that, Aunt Selma?"

"To save my life," she answered, grabbing the front of my coat and trying to pull herself over the side of the stretcher. I noticed a fresh, purple hematoma, the size of a plum, on the fragile skin of her forearm. She was staring at me with a terrified expression, her eyes either watering or crying, I couldn't tell. Then the morphine kicked in, and she let go of me and fell back on the stretcher. The orthopedic resident's serene face displayed a brief twinge of uncertainty. "I guess I'll need to get a telephone consent," he said to Fabricant, who nodded at him.

"You'll have to talk to her brother, Louis," he replied. "Nora can probably give you the phone number if it's not in the chart." Louie, my great-uncle, was Aunt Selma's only surviving brother and also a patient of Fabricant's. I gave the orthopod his number, though I had a queasy feeling. Aunt Selma obviously had no intention of consenting to the operation, at least not at the Medical Center.

As I pondered this, Fabricant ambled over to the counter in the middle of the room and sat down on a stool to write his note in her chart. The orthopedic resident went looking for a telephone. Aunt Selma was out cold, snoring gently. I followed the resident and caught up with him as he was dialing the phone.

"May I speak to him first? He's my great-uncle," I said.

"Sure," he answered cheerfully, and handed me the receiver. I dropped into a chair and waited for Uncle Louie to answer.

He sounded as if I woke him. "No, I was just reclining," he said when I asked.

"Uncle Louie, I'm in the hospital with Aunt Selma. She's OK, but she broke her hip."

There was a long silence, and then he said, "Oh boy."

"Oh boy is right."

"I'm coming," he said.

"No, don't come now. She's sleeping. They'll probably operate on her tonight or in the morning. You can come tomorrow."

He wanted to know how she had broken her hip, and I told him the little I knew, omitting her incomprehensible request to be transferred out of the Medical Center. Trying to reassure him, I said I thought Carter was a good surgeon. I had known him since my surgical clerkship as a third-year medical student, when he had been a surgical chief resident.

I told him the orthopedic resident needed to get his consent for the operation.

"Why doesn't he ask Selma?" Uncle Louie wanted to know. I explained that the resident had missed his window of opportunity, and that Aunt Selma had been rather excited. There was another pause.

"She's never been excited," he said.

Well, that was certainly the truth. In a family of mirthless stoics, Aunt Selma was among the steeliest. The best explanation I could offer was delirium secondary to all the medication she had received. "Why did they give her so much medication?" he asked. Avoiding a blatant lie, I said she was traumatized by the hip fracture and in pain. He was skeptical. We were, after all, talking about someone who had demanded, upon being told she needed all her teeth pulled, that the dentist pull them all at once so she would only miss one day of work. And that was before modern anesthesia.

I told him that I would call him back once I knew when they were taking her to the operating room.

"So, I should give the consent," he said.

"Yes, of course."

I gave the phone to the orthopedic resident, and returned to Aunt Selma's little cubicle. Michael Carter was standing next to her stretcher, talking to Fabricant, who apparently had already told him I was her niece. I doubted I had had a conversation with Carter in five years, but we often saw each other around the hospital. He said he planned to operate on Aunt Selma's hip that night, and asked the two of us to step outside of the curtain so he could examine her.

"What did they give her?" he asked.

"Let's see," said Fabricant, flipping to the medication page in the chart. "Morphine, Ativan, Haldol."

"My goodness, she's eighty-six," I groaned.

We walked back to the nursing station to wait. I was starting to feel light-headed again, and found an empty chair. The flu had an anesthetic effect, not unpleasant, that muffled the surrounding noise. Fabricant pulled up a chair next to mine and sat down to finish his pre-operative note. I thought of asking him what Aunt Selma's EKG and chest x-ray showed, but the effort seemed too great. I must have asked him though, because he answered that they were fine. He said he hadn't seen her labs yet, and got up to find an unoccupied computer terminal. Meanwhile Carter emerged from Aunt Selma's cubicle and joined me.

"Is your aunt in good health, Nora?" he asked.

I told him she was in very good health.

"I wish they hadn't sedated her so heavily," he muttered as he picked up various charts scattered on the counter, looking for hers.

"You know, it's strange. She was extremely agitated which isn't like her at all," I said.

He smiled distractedly, gave up hunting for her chart, and glanced around the emergency room for his resident. "I'm sure she'll do fine."

"Leon has the chart," I said.

He nodded. "That's fine." He had located his resident, whose name was Anthony, at the far end of the nursing station. Anthony was off the phone, so I assumed he had gotten Uncle Louie's consent. Carter signaled to him and he jumped up and rushed toward us.

Carter told the resident, who already knew it, "She's Miss Sternberg's niece."

The two conferred for a few minutes. Then Anthony got on the phone again, to the operating room this time, I supposed. Aunt Selma remained unconscious. I found a chair and dragged it behind me, setting it alongside her stretcher.

I was too queasy to move, so it seemed a good idea to sit tight and see what time they were going to take her to the OR. I peered through the opening in the curtains, absently watching the steady stream of emergency room traffic. It made me think of a renal tubule, with the cubicles along the opposite wall lined up like epithelial cells and me planted in the warm endothelium on the other shore. I was burning up. The crowd wasn't very thick for that hour of the night, yet there was a constant parade of all sorts: nurses, security guards, technicians, EMT personnel, housestaff and attending doctors, patients, family members. I had momentarily forgotten Fabricant until he leaned over me and commented that I looked sick. By then Carter was getting ready to leave the emergency department. He stopped at Aunt Selma's stretcher, and I asked him when the surgery would be.

"Now," he announced. They were getting ready to take Aunt

Selma to the operating room. You had to admire the sheer velocity of surgeons.

Carter and his resident got into their spacecraft and blasted off. The good Doctor Fabricant suggested I go home and rest. I thanked him, but lingered in Aunt Selma's cubicle. In no time it was hopping as transporters and nurses arrived to pack her up for the OR. I marveled at this, considering it always took hours, sometimes days, to get a patient up to a bed on a medical floor. I accompanied the procession down the hall to the elevators and up to the second floor entrance to the surgical suite. Aunt Selma, sharing the stretcher with the cardiac monitor, was unarousable. I watched the stretcher carry her through the swinging doors with a mix of dizziness, nausea, and anxiety.

Carter was a good orthopedic surgeon, and the anesthesiology department at Lafayette Medical Center was the best around. Aunt Selma had always loved the hospital. In that vein I consoled myself as I got back on the elevator and descended to the ground floor. I trudged back through the empty winding corridors to the main lobby.

The hospital, aside from the emergency department, had its own circadian rhythm, and was now deep in the evening shift, much quieter than in the daytime, even peaceful. Without thinking about it, I was heading home, but I realized that I had several phone calls to make and decided to get them over with. I backtracked through the lobby to the doctors' lounge, which was down a short corridor between the lobby and the atrium. Once again I swiped my ID badge, and the door to the lounge buzzed open. Directly to my left was the locked entrance to the cloakroom and beyond that the doors to the men's and women's bathrooms. In front of me was a big room with a heavy, round wooden table upon which a variety of newspapers was scattered. Armchairs, sofas, and end tables with telephones occupied two walls. Against the far wall were two laboratory computer terminals separated by a bulletin board plastered with announcements and advertisements. There was an alcove with a sink, half-refrigerator, and coffee machine, and a little table where bagels, pastries, and fruit salad were laid on weekday mornings, a vestige of a doctors' universe like a gentleman's club that existed before my time.

There was no one in the room. The television suspended from the wall was tuned to a basketball game. I took a pint of skim milk from the refrigerator and dropped into one of the armchairs. Brad thought that milk made a cold worse. But he wasn't a doctor, was he? I pulled a telephone into my lap and dialed it.

The first call was to Uncle Louie, to tell him Aunt Selma was going into surgery. He said, "I've been thinking about what you told me, and I'm not sure I should have given the consent."

I felt a rollicking wave of nausea. "You had to, Uncle Louie," I pleaded. "She has to have her hip fixed. There's no alternative."

"So why didn't she give the consent? It's so unlike her. Was she mixed up?"

"Not exactly," I said. "They gave her a lot of medicine, and I think it affected her. But you did the right thing."

"I hope so," he said. Uncle Louie sounded unconvinced. We agreed that I would meet him in the hospital lobby in the morning.

I called my cousin Inez in Hoboken. Her relationship to Aunt Selma was parallel to mine: We were both granddaughters of Selma's deceased older brothers. However, as I reminded myself in the throes of an escalating temperature, I was not only grandfatherless, but grandmotherless and parentless as well, whereas she still had her mother.

Inez already knew about Aunt Selma, having just spoken to her mother, my father's first cousin Charlotte, who had gotten it from Uncle Louie.

"So why did Uncle Louie have to give the consent for surgery? He's all shook up about it, you know," Inez said. I told her about Aunt Selma's unexpected agitation. "So why's that?" she asked. I sank deeper into the chair and closed my eyes. I wished Inez wouldn't drill me. I pictured her attacking the jet black curtain of bangs that hung over her eyebrows, flicking them around with the fingers of her right hand, something she did when she was vexed. I replied that I didn't know why Aunt Selma was agitated, but that it wasn't unusual for old people to become confused when they were sick or traumatized. "Uh-huh," she said. I hated to have to explain anything remotely medical to her, because I hated that "Uh-huh."

"Is she OK?" Inez asked.

"I think so. The surgery is tonight."

"I'm going to drive my mother and Uncle Louie in to see her tomorrow. You sound terrible."

I heard the door to the lounge open. My head was too heavy to turn around. Inez asked if I was still at the hospital. I told her I was going home shortly but coming back early in the morning. She said she would call her brother, my cousin Peter, in Phoenix, and that Charlotte was calling our great-aunt in Los Angeles and a few of Aunt Selma's nephews and nieces scattered around the country, to inform them. That covered the first-circle, from which the news would radiate.

We hung up, and I stretched out in the chair and had a whopping rigor. The door to the lounge swung open and shut softly, as if it were far away. I stared blankly ahead at the jumble of notices tacked on the bulletin board: office space for rent, a Grand Rounds schedule, a sign-up sheet for new hospital ID badges, a fancy invitation to the dinner honoring Dr. Griffin Garrett for fifty years of service to the Medical Center. The sounds of the basketball game became blurry. The chair was irresistible, and I fell asleep.

I dreamed I was leaving the Museum of Natural History: Night was falling, and I realized I had no apartment to go home to. Suddenly I was walking down Schilling Three and a crowd of people lined the walls, reading newspapers. Some of them were talking to themselves. There was a code going on in the room I was approaching. House officers strolled in and out, also reading something, I couldn't tell what. The angel of death, wearing khaki pants and a crewneck sweater and holding a visitor's pass, leaned unobtrusively in the doorway. His face was turned inward so I couldn't see it. I walked toward the room, but I never got any closer, and then I was in an airport, drifting past huge empty windows.

When I woke up, about half an hour had passed. My throat felt like I had swallowed a gauze pad, and I discovered I had had a nosebleed. I washed my face in the bathroom and called the operating suite. I asked if Aunt Selma had gone in for her surgery yet and was told they had just wheeled her in.

Knowing I wouldn't be able to see her for the next few hours, I left the hospital and walked back to West One Hundred and Sixth Street. A light snow was falling, dampening the noises of the street. When an empty cab cruised by I toppled in, though there were only four blocks to go. By the time I got to my building, I was carsick to boot. The unfurnished, uncarpeted lobby, always garish under its fluorescent lighting, was empty, and I was relieved not to have to talk to anyone. I rode the elevator to the fifth floor and stumbled into my apartment and into bed, stopping only for two extra-strength Tylenol from a bottle I found on the bedroom floor, and a glass of water.

Brad had called from his hotel at about 1:00 A.M., but I slept through it, as I learned later in the morning when I listened to the answering machine. At 6:00 A.M. the phone rang again, and I awakened. It was Leon Fabricant, to tell me that Aunt Selma was dead.

CHAPTER TWO

Leon Fabricant accepted his patient's death with admirable fortitude. I suppose Aunt Selma's advanced age made it easier, but I had to wonder if he ever sweated anything about a patient. He couldn't answer any of my questions, obvious as they were. All he knew was that the surgery had gone well, she was stable in the recovery room and doing fine on the orthopedic floor until someone noticed she was dead.

"You know what her advance directives were," he said, referring to Aunt Selma's wish not to be resuscitated.

"It's what she said would happen," I whispered in amazement.

"What do you mean?"

"You remember, that's why they had to knock her out in the ER. She was hysterical. She kept saying she was going to die."

He didn't say anything for a moment, then he spat out, "Nora, she was delirious, she was eighty-two!"

"Was she on heparin?" I asked.

"I don't know. I understand how upset you are. It's terribly upsetting."

"I'd like to know more of the details."

He suggested I speak directly to Michael Carter, who had notified him of Aunt Selma's death. As soon as I hung up the phone I called the hospital operator and asked for Carter's office number. She connected me to his answering service, and in ten minutes he called back.

Carter, at least, showed a modicum of decent regret over Aunt Selma's death, probably because he had wielded the knife. She had done beautifully, he informed me, intra-operatively and in the immediate post-operative period. He could only speculate that she had had a cardiac arrhythmia, or perhaps a pulmonary embolism, even though she had been appropriately prophylaxed. In fact, it sounded like everything had been done correctly. I remembered how meticulous he had been as chief resident.

"Your aunt was a great lady, wasn't she?" he asked.

"Yes."

"The nurses in the recovery room couldn't get over her. She entertained them with stories about the hospital from fifty years ago."

"She was there."

"I'm very sorry, Nora."

I thanked him and hung up. As I sat on the edge of the bed, I pictured Aunt Selma reaching out to grab me in the emergency room. An arctic draft rattled the dirty Venetian blinds in the window.

I was dripping with sweat. It wasn't their fault they were dirty, I never cleaned them. I switched off the lamp next to the bed and tried to lie down again.

After a minute, I turned the light back on, opened the drawer of the night table and pulled out a scrap of paper with an unusually long telephone number. It took two tries to dial it correctly. The ring was melodious and even sounded like it came from another country. When the hotel clerk picked up, I asked for Brad Goodwin and was told that Mr. Goodwin had gone out. I had forgotten it was afternoon in Norway, and Brad would be at work in the theater. I left a message. Then I dialed the hospital operator again and asked to be connected to the nursing station on Seven North. Eventually, I was connected to the charge nurse, who introduced herself as Mary Louise. I gave her my name, said I was Selma Sternberg's niece, and that I would be coming right to the hospital. Mary Louise said they would keep Aunt Selma in her room until I got there.

A wave of nausea swept though me. I hung up the phone and bent forward on the edge of the bed. Then I started to dial Uncle Louie but hung up midway. Breaking the news to him ought to be done carefully. I felt like my head was going to crack in half as I heaved myself out of bed to search for the Tylenol bottle. I couldn't remember where I had put it down in my obtunded state the night before. The living room, at the back of the apartment, was a blurry gray in the ethereal light that filtered through the corner windows. I stood for a while in the middle of the room, blankly surveying the black rooftops of a sea of old buildings, and beyond those, in the distance, a tiny colorless bar of the Hudson River. Everything was the same, except that I had acquired a new permanent loss, a space-occupying emptiness, a miserable tenant I could never evict.

I couldn't find the Tylenol, but I came across some Pepto-Bismol in the kitchen so I took that. The thing to do was to call Charlotte, who lived in East Brunswick, a few miles from Uncle Louie, and have her tell him in person.

Charlotte sounded braced for bad news. Her reaction was typically Sternberg, unflinching and unquestioning. She would go to Uncle Louie's house right away. And she would call Inez. The inevitable sequence of communications and arrangements was that easily launched.

I shoved my clothes on and was looking around the kitchen for my keys when the phone rang. Inez wanted to know if she should meet me at the hospital. I told her it wasn't necessary. She was going to drive to her mother's house and would wait for me if I wanted to take a train to Hoboken and go with her. I thanked her but declined the offer. In that case she would bundle up Charles, her fifteen month-old son, and go. Her husband Stuart would drive down when he got out of work. Stuart was a stockbroker on Wall Street. She suggested I accompany him, or if I could come sooner, that I take a train and someone would pick me up at the New Brunswick station. I told her I was going to the hospital, and when I returned to my apartment I was going to lie down for the rest of the day and night. There was a silence.

"When is Brad coming home?" she asked

"In about six weeks."

"So you're going to just stay there, alone in your apartment?"

"Yep."

She was displeased. "Well, call me at my mother's if you change your mind. Or at Uncle Louie's, it's more likely we'll be there."

I hung up the phone and swayed dizzily. When the lightheadedness had passed, I gathered up my coat from the kitchen chair where I had dropped it the night before and headed back to the hospital. Either it was colder outside than before or I was less feverish. The icy air in my throat triggered a prolonged spasm of coughing. People walking by on the sidewalk probably thought I had tuberculosis.

When I reached Seven North, the orthopedic floor, I was informed by the unit clerk that Aunt Selma had just been sent downstairs.

"But Mary Louise said they would keep her on the floor until I got here," I protested. A tall, dark-haired woman in a nurse's uniform, standing behind the receptionist, lifted her head from the chart she was holding and said, "I'm Mary Louise. I'm sorry I couldn't keep her here."

"What happened?" I asked.

"We needed the bed and Dr. Zahn said we should move her."

"Who's Dr. Zahn?"

"He's the orthopedic resident."

I considered whether I should ask for his beeper and page him, or call Michael Carter back, or do neither. I sensed that my decision making capacity was grinding to a halt. Why such efficiency? It always took so long to move a living, or even a half-dead patient around the hospital.

"Would you like to pick up her belongings?" Mary Louise asked.

I nodded.

"You have to go down to admitting."

"Admitting?" I said. "She's dead. It's the opposite of Admitting. It's the ultimate Discharging." I sneezed spasmodically, dropping almost to my knees.

Mary Louise looked at me sympathetically. "That's where the safe is," she explained.

I wiped my nose with a handful of tissues from my pocket. "OK," I said weakly.

"I'm sorry."

I headed back to the elevator bank. Two elevators arrived together, one releasing a voluble, over-caffeinated crowd of interns and medical students, all dressed in green surgical scrubs under white coats, hurrying somewhere, probably to rounds. I stumbled into the other one, which was empty, and hesitated after the door closed. There was nothing stopping me from going down to the cold room to find Aunt Selma, except that I felt faint contemplating it. It was what I ought to do, and I pressed the button for the sub-basement. The elevator stopped on the first floor and a few people in civilian clothes started to get on. "I'm going down," I said, without irony, and they retreated.

When the door opened at the sub-basement, I stepped out and looked up and down the long cinderblock corridor illuminated by a succession of yellow lights mounted on a low ceiling. It reminded me of the Lincoln Tunnel without the tiles. Since finishing residency

I hadn't had much occasion to wander through the bowels of the hospital, and I couldn't remember the direction to the cold room. There was no sign indicating the way, so I turned left. I had rounded one corner and started down another stretch of the corridor when I saw Walter Fish, the renowned kidney pathologist, approaching. I had worked on one of his many research projects when I was a medical student.

"Hi, Nora," he said, smiling and stopping in front of me. He wasn't much taller than I, maybe five-foot-five, overweight, with thinning gray hair and silver eyeglasses. His most memorable feature, though, was his prosthetic left eye. Many people found it disconcerting to converse with Walter because of it. You had to stay focused on the right eye, but the temptation to glance at the inert thing in the left socket could be overpowering. Myths abounded at medical school to explain its origin.

"What brings you to the underworld?" he asked.

"I'm looking for the cold room," I said.

"The cold room?" He stopped smiling. "What for?"

I wanted to give a brief, nonspecific answer, but nothing came to mind. I said, "My great-aunt died in the hospital this morning, after hip surgery, and they've already brought her body down here, and I feel like I should look at it." We stared at each other, both of us surprised.

"I'm sorry, Nora," he said. "How terrible."

I started sneezing again.

"And you're sick," he observed. I nodded, my nose once more deep in tissues. "How old was your aunt?"

"Eighty-six."

"Had she been ill?"

"No," I said. "She just fractured her hip."

He looked at me kindly with his right eye. "May I ask if there's going to be a post-mortem?"

"A post-mortem," I echoed. How could I not even consider that? "It hadn't crossed my mind. What could I have been thinking?"

"Well, not everyone has to have one," he said quickly, waving his hands in front of him. "I was thinking more in terms of what preparations might be going on, whether she might be in the morgue." The hospital morgue, separate from the cold room, was where autopsies were performed. "Nora, you're not expected to be the one that brings that up when you're a family member," he continued.

No, of course not, it should have been Leon, I thought. But Leon had already written Aunt Selma off. I, on the other hand, would have liked to know the exact cause of death. I recognized, however, that requesting an autopsy was a moot point. Uncle Louie was officially the next of kin, so he would have to give his consent, and I couldn't imagine that.

"I know," I sighed. He put his hand on my upper arm, and in a soft voice said, "Nora, I would suggest that you don't go into the cold room. It's a hard place to see someone you knew. It's too bad you weren't able to see her while she was on the floor." When I didn't say anything he added, "If you'd like, I'll walk over to the cold room and make sure everything's in order. Would that help?"

There was no reason why it should, yet it was a bizarrely comforting offer. "Thank you, Dr. Fish. Yes, I think it would help." It might have been my imagination, but it looked like his prosthesis was listing slightly laterally and inferiorly. I focused intently on the other eye.

"Certainly. I'll let you know if there is anything to be concerned about. You were headed in the right direction, by the way. It's just a little farther down the hall, past the next corner to the right."

I watched him retrace his steps until he was out of sight. Then I walked back to the elevator. I ascended to the first floor and cut across a corner of the atrium to the lobby. The admitting office was located down a short corridor that branched off the lobby next to the ATM machine. I passed through the glass door and entered a line in front of a counter where clerks stood at individual stations next to computer terminals. The line moved slowly, but finally I was able to collect Aunt Selma's belongings. They were handed to me in a clear plastic shopping bag decorated with the hospital logo, a Colonial figure looking through a small telescope. In the bag, indifferently exposed, as if to commemorate the patient's last hours in a skimpy hospital gown, were the few items Aunt Selma had on her when she was brought to the Emergency Department: her pocketbook, eyeglasses, and wristwatch.

The admitting clerk handed me a receipt to sign as I leaned against the counter, and a form requesting the name and address of the funeral home. She asked if I had been offered an opportunity to speak to a chaplain. She said it the way the cashier at the drugstore asks if you found everything you were looking for. I said no, I hadn't, so she asked if I would like to speak to one. I said no again, and she picked up a pen and made a notation on a form in front of her. "OK, thank you," she said.

I knew without a doubt what she was doing. It had to be some customer satisfaction improvement initiative that the hospital had cooked up as part of its highly-publicized "Taking the Temperature of Excellence" campaign. It all seemed awfully unceremonious, I thought, almost tawdry, as I stuffed the shopping bag under my arm and headed back to the lobby. Forty-odd years toiling in the hospital and that's what you get.

I wasn't ready to go home, so I stepped into the atrium. This was the large, vaulted space behind the lobby, crowned with skylights and containing real trees and vines, a waterfall, and a coffee shop. There was an escalator at either end, like in a department store, leading to a mezzanine. I sat down at one of the little tables between the trees, laid my head down on my arms, and remained in that position until someone tapped me on the shoulder. I looked up to see Jessica, holding a styrofoam cup of coffee in her left hand, her right arm supporting a cardboard box, and her overstuffed briefcase slung across her shoulder.

"Nora, what are you doing?" she asked.

"I'm disintegrating," I said.

"You look awful. Why are you here? Why aren't you home?" She set the cardboard box down on the table, pulled out the chair across from me, dumped her briefcase on the floor, and sat down. She had on her white coat, as usual, over a brown turtleneck sweater and plaid woolen skirt. Her brown hair was clasped in a barrette at the back of her neck.

I told her about Aunt Selma, in detail. When I was finished, I said, "What's killing me is that she knew she was going to die. She asked me to help her, to save her, really, and I didn't do it."

Jessica grimaced. "That's absurd. She was—how old, in her eighties?"

I nodded as I pulled some tissues out of my pocket and sneezed noisily.

"The reason she knew she could die is because she knew she was about to have a big operation." She said this with characteristic forcefulness.

"Not could die," I corrected her, "would die. And it had to do with being at the Medical Center."

"I thought your aunt revered the Medical Center."

"So did I."

"Nora, your aunt was a nurse. She understood the risks. I don't know what she said about Mother Lafayette, but between the trauma and the meds, she was probably delirious."

"Well, we'll never know, will we?" *Piloerection*, I thought, looking at my arms which had broken out in goose bumps. Jessica leaned across the table and put the back of her hand against my forehead.

"You've got a fever," she said.

"Do I? Well, I'm going home." I stood abruptly, which proved to be a miscalculation, and slid back into the chair.

"Do you want me to tell Irwin about your aunt, and that you'll be out longer?" She meant my boss Irwin Liu, director of the Lafayette Primary Care Internal Medicine Clinic, or PCIMC, where I worked as one of the attending physicians. Like every teaching hospital, Lafayette had an out-patient clinic where the medical residents were exposed to the practice of primary care, specifically the care of indigent patients from the surrounding neighborhoods. Since the status of doctors at the Medical Center was directly related to the status of their patients in society, the PCIMC doctors were the plankton-eaters on the hospital food chain, the poor plankton themselves being the doctors in the primary care pediatrics clinic.

Jessica also worked full time at the hospital, as an endocrinologist. We had been medical school classmates, class of 1983, and residents together, then Jessica had gone on to do an Endocrinology fellowship at the Medical Center while I started at PCIMC. Our other good friend from medical school, Celine Byrd, had done a residency in psychiatry, also at Lafayette, and for the past year had been the director of the in-patient psychiatry unit.

"Irwin doesn't expect me back until next week, anyway," I said. "What are you carrying around?" I looked in the cardboard box. It contained rubber-banded stacks of patient information about diabetes and cholesterol in English and Spanish, packages of coupons from a pharmaceutical company for discounted diabetes medication, a bag of plastic odometers, splashy colored pens imprinted with pharmaceutical logos, similarly marked plastic measuring cups, and boxes of sample medications.

"It's all for the diabetes fair. I'm scrounging freebies from the drug companies. You know I'm shameless." Jessica always had at least one patient-oriented project going on the side in addition to her clinical practice and her research, which was in osteoporosis, and for this year, the rotating presidency of the medical staff. The diabetes fair was one of her favorite activities, for which she lined up various local organizations and clinics, extracted money from pharmaceutical companies who would push their wares, and secured space from Lafayette, which would reap the public relations benefit. Generally she and I referred to donations from pharmaceutical manufacturers as "blood money," basking in our virtuousness as we turned down fancy dinners, but we counted these events as exceptions.

"Look, this was a real coup," she said, pulling out a box of chemstrips, the expensive strips of paper used to test blood sugar. "I got one of the glucometer manufacturers to donate 100 boxes."

"You're planning on giving them out to uninsured patients?" I said.

"Of course."

"But the hospital's not going to let them past the gate."

She shrugged. "How will they know? Anyway, Van Dyke is going to be there, and they can always use stuff like this." The Van Dyke West Side Community Health Center was a scandal-ridden independent clinic located on the outer fringe of Lafayette's catchment area, where another of our friends from residency, Eugene Velazquez, practiced. The doctors at Van Dyke used Lafayette when they needed to admit their patients to the hospital, and Lafayette used Van Dyke as a site to train their medical students and residents. Otherwise the two institutions had little to do with each other.

I stood again, slowly, picked up the bag of Aunt Selma's belongings, and said I was going home to bed.

Jessica offered to walk outside with me and hail a cab, but I insisted I could manage and veered off unsteadily in the direction of the lobby. As I passed the last tree in the atrium, Michael Carter overtook me, gently laying his hand on my arm.

"I'm sorry, Nora," he said. "I had planned to call you this morning, before you called me."

"That's all right." I replied. We stood facing each other, awkwardly. We had both been trained to give bad news, to tell a patient's family that despite all our efforts their loved one had died. We were experienced in saying that we had tried our best, and that our best was insufficient. Yet neither of us knew what to say.

"I was just going home," I told him, gesturing toward the lobby.

"Yeah, OK," he said. "If you have any questions later, if you want to talk to me about anything, just call me."

I thanked him and continued toward the main entrance. A clammy sweat coated my chest and the back of my neck, and I was shivering. I completed more than one circuit in the revolving door and was at risk of being spectacularly embarrassed as the security guard edged forward to help me, when I spun out to the pavement. I glanced back loftily at the door, drew myself up to my full height of five-feet-three inches, and swerved forward, tacking north.

The air was refreshingly cold. Wavelets of icy wind currents propelled me away from the hospital and up the bright avenue, where the sunlight stung my eyes. When I reached the corner opposite my building, I stopped at the Korean market to buy a carton of orange juice and added it to my Lafayette bag. I seemed to cross the street in slow motion as traffic bore down on me, until finally I climbed the concrete steps and pushed open the heavy glass door to the lobby of my building.

One of my neighbors, a man about my age whom I occasionally saw coming in and out of the building wearing a baseball cap declaring "World Peace," was taping hand-written signs with the same message on the walls, reminding me that we were at war. He had written a little speech in defense of peace that he attempted to deliver at every opportunity, sometimes in song. Like our other neighbors, I had already listened to it, and I gave him wide berth although I agreed with his position. Luckily, this time his back was turned, and I slipped quietly into the empty elevator. As it crept upward I opened the orange juice carton and took a long draught. Once inside my apartment I shed my coat on the hall floor and fell into bed.

It was already dark when the phone rang and woke me up. Inez was calling to tell me the funeral would be the next day, in New Brunswick. Aunt Selma would be buried in Piscataway, New Jersey, at Clairmont, the Sternberg cemetery of choice. Inez had made all the arrangements. She was handing out assignments and wanted to know if I felt up to receiving one. I said I did, and she charged me with picking up our great-aunt Tootsie at Newark Airport the next morning and bringing her to the funeral home.

I got back in bed but couldn't sleep. I had that thermo-disregulated, disoriented feeling I remembered from the waking day/night/day cycles of residency. I couldn't shake the image of Aunt Selma on her stretcher in the ER because I didn't believe it was delirium that had agitated her. It was something about the Medical Center, but I'd be damned if I knew what.

There was no denying that I had left her to die in the hospital, as she predicted she would. I was trapped in this rumination when Brad called, and I spilled the whole story, hardly stopping for air. Like Jessica, he thought my anxiety was groundless. Brad said he regretted he couldn't be at the funeral, and I appreciated that, though I knew it wasn't true. He was squeamish about other people's deaths and funerals, though he remarked from time to time that he looked forward to his own.

I asked him how he was enjoying Norway, and he heaped praise on the pristine, bracing air, the state-subsidized theater, and the herring. He went so far as to suggest that we move there, but I knew he would fit in better than I, Viking-like in appearance as he was. After we hung up, I felt, for the first time in days, like eating something. I went to the kitchen, imagining herring, but the closest thing I could find was a can of tuna fish, so I opened that.

CHAPTER THREE

Aunt Tootsie's plane from Los Angeles was two hours late, ruling out our appearance at the funeral home. We had to proceed directly to the cemetery, and she took this in stride.

Aunt Tootsie was now the oldest surviving Sternberg sibling. There had been eight of them: Istvan, who had died in some horrible horse and carriage accident in Budapest; Oscar, Inez and Peter's grandfather; Harry, my grandfather; Selma; the three diminutives: Aunts Tootsie, Bunny, and Cookie (a.k.a. Florence, Bella, and Sadie); and Uncle Louie.

As we bumped along in the back of the airport taxi, Aunt Tootsie updated me on my various cousins in Los Angeles. Everyone was surprised to hear that Aunt Selma had died "out of the blue," which was totally medically incorrect.

Then she asked me, "Has anyone told Bunny?" For a moment I didn't know what she was talking about. She looked at me with a very serious, almost grim expression as we struggled not to tumble into each other's laps while the cab rocked and lurched.

"My sister Bunny," she elaborated.

I was ashamed that I hadn't thought at all of Aunt Bunny, or "poor Bunny" as my mother called her on those infrequent occasions when she was discussed within my hearing. "I don't know," I said.

"Well, I certainly think someone should." I wondered why she didn't volunteer, but I was too intimidated to ask. I knew so little about Aunt Bunny, really nothing beyond the fact that she had been institutionalized as a young adult. During my psychiatry rotation in medical school I had asked my father to tell me her diagnosis, but he only answered that she was very nervous. "Nervous" was the Sternberg code word for insane. I had never met her, and she had been a taboo subject all my life.

"I'm embarrassed to say I don't know where Aunt Bunny is," I stammered.

Tootsie scowled. "She's at Vista View Rest Home in New Haven," she said. "Been there for twenty-eight years."

"New Haven?" I echoed, astonished. There was something incongruous about a Sternberg in Connecticut. "What's she doing in New Haven?"

Aunt Tootsie said, "Nora, didn't your parents tell you anything about the Bunny situation?"

"No, hardly anything," I answered. After an awkward pause I added, "I didn't know there was a situation."

She shook her head and murmured, "They were so loyal, your parents," and she started to cry soundlessly. She attacked her pocketbook with trembling hands as the taxi flung us forward and back, and I surmised that she wanted a tissue. I handed her a package from my own pocketbook, and she took a few and dabbed around her eyes. "Bunny was very nervous," she said. "Not always, of course. It didn't start until she was about twenty-four." She paused and blew her nose. "They say your great-grandfather was the same age."

"As what?" I asked, not following.

"When he developed, you know, problems."

"No, I don't know," I insisted. "My great-grandfather, you mean your father?"

She nodded. She rolled her head, with its soft cover of white waves, against the maroon vinyl of the taxi upholstery, closing her eyes. With her sharply etched mouth and high cheekbones she wasn't frail looking, none of them had ever been, even those who managed to march north of ninety. But she looked exhausted, and I was torn between the instinct to leave her alone, and the curiosity that she had awakened to plumb the Sternberg depths. What was I likely to learn? That some of us undoubtedly carried genes for schizophrenia, or perhaps mania, and that the phenotype tended to emerge at age 24? Did that mean that I was safe, at 33, or could I be a late bloomer? And where there was mental illness there was certain to be an abundance of lies, guilt, and grief. Was this the detour I wanted to take on the way to Aunt Selma's funeral? Actually, I yearned to go there, but it seemed too cruel to drag Aunt Tootsie along.

We rode on in silence down the turnpike. After a while, she started up the conversation again in her usual, businesslike manner, asking about Brad, whom the Sternbergs consistently called "Greg." I explained that Brad was in Norway, directing *King Lear*. Aunt Tootsie commented that it was a good thing I hadn't gone with him.

At last we arrived at the cemetery to find the small funeral party already gathered at the gravesite, the coffin already in the ground. I would have estimated the median age of the mourners to be about 65. While I paid the driver, Aunt Tootsie popped out of the cab and was immediately engulfed by her nieces and nephews. They swept her over the frozen grass to the inner circle by the grave. She hugged Uncle Louie and the two linked arms and stood together squinting up at the brilliant sun, straight-backed and stoic.

I had relieved Aunt Tootsie of her suitcase and placed it in the trunk of Stuart's car, as instructed. As I hurried toward the assemblage I kept my head down to respectfully avoid seeing more of Clairmont, for the moment, at least, than I had to. I was overly familiar with this unfeeling landscape, crowded with headstones, among them my parents'. Standing around the grave, we huddled and shivered, everyone's breath visible in the biting sunshine. The service was over quickly, and the group began to disperse, treading hesitantly over the icy ground.

The rabbi walked a few paces behind the departing cars, and then climbed into the back seat of a station wagon with several elderly men from Aunt Selma's synagogue who were driving back to Manhattan. He rolled down the window as Uncle Louie approached and bent over to speak to them, thanking them for making the trip, no doubt. Uncle Louie was six feet tall and thin, smartly dressed, as always, wearing black pants, a gray herringbone overcoat, and a solid gray scarf. His gait was brisk and energetic and he could apparently still flex his back without difficulty. Yet as he stooped to rest his arm on the edge of the passenger window, he looked to me like an old man.

I lingered by the graveside. The stone stood half-concealed under a black drape. There under the ground was Aunt Selma in her coffin, lifting up her arms to grab me. What a sick thought, I reproached myself. I walked back to the road and stumbled on the slippery path, nearly falling when an impudent squirrel darted in front of me. Weren't they supposed to be sleeping in dens under trees or something? Inez, coming up behind me, grabbed my arm.

"Are you all right?" she asked. Before I could answer, she turned to tell Peter the seating arrangements for the ride to Uncle Louie's house, where most of us were headed. Peter was four years younger than Inez and used to taking orders from her. He was unshaven and looked a little punchy, having arrived, like Aunt Tootsie, just hours before on the red-eye. Aunt Tootsie and I were now separated. She rode with Uncle Louie, Peter, and Charlotte in Charlotte's Taurus. I was in Stuart's Volvo with Inez, Stuart, our cousin Stanley, who was late Aunt Cookie's son, and his wife Frances. Stanley and Frances had flown in from West Palm Beach. As the car crawled along the narrow road to the cemetery gates, Stanley reminisced about Aunt Selma. He recalled that he had last seen her at his grandson Maxim's Bar Mitzvah the year before. Speaking of his grandchildren, Maxim's sister, Audrey, he informed us, had just been accepted at Brown University.

Frances asked if Aunt Selma had been sick, and I told her that she had been very well, as far as I knew, until she fell.

"You know, this is the second funeral we've been to in a month," Stanley said, "and come to think of it, the last one was after an operation, too."

"It was?" Frances asked.

"Of course. Hadn't he just had an arthroscopy on his knee?"

"Who are you talking about?" Inez asked, craning her neck to look at us in the back seat.

Stanley explained, "My former urologist, Sheldon Pomerantz, went in for an arthroscopy, and died on the table."

"Well," I said, "dying after hip surgery is one thing. But dying after arthroscopy is really unheard of."

No one said anything.

"What hospital was he in?" I asked.

"Your hospital," Stanley said, "nothing personal." I looked at him closely to see if he was joking, but he appeared to be perfectly serious. He bore a striking resemblance to Uncle Louie. They had the same mustard-colored skin, and although he had to be in his late sixties, Stanley had a full head of the wavy, jet-black hair that distinguished a Sternberg.

"Where was the funeral, in Florida?" Inez asked.

"No, here, well not here, out on the island."

"Way out," Frances added. Though an in-law, she shared the Sternbergs' New Jersey identification and was inclined to cast a cold eye on Long Island.

"You flew up for your former urologist's funeral?" Inez asked. Frances answered that they were already here for her brother's seventieth birthday.

There wasn't too much conversation after that. We all seemed troubled by the revelation about Stanley's urologist. I felt positively nauseated, though I wasn't sure if it was the anecdote or motion sickness or the flu. In any event, it was a relief to step out of the car at Uncle Louie's house, where we were the first to arrive.

Inez had brought Charlotte's key, and she let us in through the back porch, really a vestibule, that led to the kitchen. The house was a brown brick Cape Cod, situated at the top of a street of similarly modest houses. There was a long, narrow backyard rimmed on two sides with azaleas, shrunken and dusted with snow, and enclosed by a wire fence that provided a run for Uncle Louie's dog. He, Rex, a mixture of collie and other large breeds, received us joyfully at the back door. Lucky Rex, I thought, who didn't know he wouldn't see Aunt Selma again. Also awaiting us, stacked on the steps leading to the porch, were two cardboard boxes containing saran-wrapped platters of food from the nearby Jerusalem Famous Delicatessen. The bearers of whitefish salad, food of death, had lost no time.

"Move over, Rex," Stuart grunted, carrying in one of the boxes and setting it on the kitchen table. Stanley followed with the second box.

"Hi, Rexy," Inez murmured, bending over to scratch his neck. He immediately rolled onto his back, all four legs pointing at the ceiling.

Stuart collected our coats and paraphernalia, and Inez installed Frances and Stanley on the living room sofa, admonishing Rex, who was sniffing their legs, to leave them alone. She then sent Stuart to the basement to bring up folding chairs, and returned to the kitchen to start setting up the food. I sat with Frances and Stanley for a few minutes, sneezing and blowing my nose, until Frances said they wouldn't be offended if I went to lie down somewhere. I thanked her and retreated upstairs to the spare bedroom, thinking I would just rest on the bed for a few minutes.

Four hours later I was awakened by the shriek of a teakettle. I stood up and heard a pained yelp. I had stepped on Rex, who was lying on the floor beside the bed, invisible in the darkness. Groping for the lamp on the little rolltop desk, I switched on the light and was surprised to see that the door to the room was closed. I squatted down and stroked Rex's back, causing his tail to gyrate and thump the floor. "They closed you in here with me, Rex," I said. I stood up, reeling a little, and grabbed the edge of the desk to steady myself. "What's this?" I said out loud. As soon as I heard my voice I added, "I'm asking you, Rex." Given my gene pool, I thought it was a good idea not to talk to myself.

A photograph lay in the center of the desk. I wondered as I picked it up how I could have missed it earlier. In my hand was a black and white snapshot of four young women standing side by side in front of a treeless expanse of grass. A row of hilltops was just distinguishable in the distance. All four wore loose dresses with large collars, and three had on hats. They were sisters. The one on the far right, the only one with curly hair, was Aunt Cookie, and I could pick out Aunt Tootsie and Aunt Selma in the middle. Aunt Selma had linked arms with the one to her left, who was looking away from the camera, the one without a hat, the one who had to be Aunt Bunny.

It was the first time I had ever seen a picture of her. She was without a doubt the prettiest of the four. Doesn't that just figure, I thought. Uncle Louie had probably taken out the picture to look at it sometime in the last forty-eight hours. It hadn't occurred to me before that there might be pictures of my unknown aunt. I wondered how many more existed, and who had them. I had never seen any in Aunt Selma's apartment. The notion to search the drawers of the rolltop desk flitted across my mind, but I would never have violated my uncle's privacy like that. The idea was repugnant.

I opened the drawers one by one. Except for a pencil, they were empty. I replaced the photograph in the center of the desk and sat down on the bed. Rex sat at my feet.

I *had* seen a picture of Aunt Bunny before. I just hadn't known it was her. In my parents' house, among a collection of framed photographs arranged on the bookshelves in the den, was a picture of my mother as a young woman with one of my father's aunts. I had always assumed it was Aunt Tootsie, but now that I had seen the other picture, I knew I had been wrong. The two figures, about the same height, were standing in front of a windowless white wall, my mother's arm around Aunt Bunny's shoulder. A single metal chair stood behind them. My mother had her face turned toward Aunt Bunny and she smiled. Aunt Bunny looked at the floor.

The picture, like everything else that remained from my parents' house, was in my possession. I had saved all the memorabilia and photographs, packed in cardboard boxes that Brad had neatly labeled and stored in the second bedroom in our apartment. The day would probably come when I would be ready to look through them.

I patted Rex on the head and the two of us went downstairs. All the guests had left, excluding Peter, who was staying for a few days at his mother's house, and Aunt Tootsie, who would spend the week at Uncle Louie's. I wandered into the kitchen and found Charlotte washing dishes and Inez making a cup of tea for Aunt Tootsie. Charlotte asked what I would like to eat. I took a cup of coffee into the living room where Aunt Tootsie and Uncle Louie were hanging tough. Peter, sprawled on the sofa, was asleep. Rex lay on the floor next to Uncle Louie. No one said much, but there was nothing extraordinary in that. Had Aunt Cookie or Uncle Oscar, prolific authors of doggerel, still been with us there would have been recitations, but none of the living was inclined in that direction. After we sat awhile longer Inez walked in from the kitchen and said she and Stuart were leaving and would drop me at the PATH train in Hoboken. When I rose to get my coat Uncle Louie jumped up and followed me to the hall closet.

He said in a low voice, as he handed me my coat, "I've been thinking about Selma's odd behavior in the emergency room."

I had wondered whether he had forgotten about the emergency room. "Yes?" I said.

"I hate to think I gave the consent to…well, but if she could have given the consent, she would have, right?"

"You had to do it. There was no alternative," I said.

"So I think she must have gotten too much medication. Otherwise she would have done it."

"She was knocked out."

"That's what I think."

"It was the right thing to do."

"OK," he said, "we're finished."

"We're finished?"

"Yeah, that's it."

"What do you mean?" I asked. "I can't think about it any more if I want to?"

"There's nothing else to think about."

"Well, what if I want to mull it over some more?"

"Why would you?"

Why, indeed. Because unlike the rest of them, I possessed the capacity for self-doubt.

Uncle Louie returned to the living room with a lighter step. I followed him, said goodbye to Aunt Tootsie, and then headed through the kitchen to the back door. Charlotte tried to send me off with a Tupperware of leftover whitefish, which I could have carried like a talisman through the tunnels of the PATH train and the subways, but I resisted.

By the time I got home it was hours past my usual bed time, yet I was wide awake. It wasn't quite late enough to call Brad. I got in bed and started reading a review article on memory dysfunction in the *Archives of Internal Medicine*. That did the trick.

CHAPTER FOUR

When the prescribed week of mourning was over, Aunt Tootsie returned to Los Angeles. The Sunday after she left, Uncle Louie, Charlotte, Inez, and I met at Aunt Selma's apartment to begin the sad task of emptying it. The three of them drove in from New Jersey in Charlotte's car, which they had loaded with trash bags and boxes. Miraculously, they found a parking spot right in front of Aunt Selma's building. It was a mild, windless February day, and I decided to walk the twenty-four blocks downtown to West Eighty-second Street. Since rigid punctuality was encoded in our DNA, we converged at the entrance to the apartment building at the appointed hour, 9:00 A.M., on the dot.

Originally, Stuart was to join us in a rental truck, but Inez had been unable to find a babysitter, so Stuart had to stay home with Charles. Inez explained this to me as we rode the elevator up to the eighth floor. The familiar warm smell of the landing, of something eternally baking, enveloped us as we emerged and crossed the little square hall. We each rustled our pockets or pocketbooks for the keys, saying almost in unison, "I've got it." Uncle Louie produced his first and opened the door. Inside, the apartment was, predictably, the same as it had always been. I don't know what I had expected. No one said anything, and it was as quiet as if we had never entered, since of course no one else was there. After a moment, Uncle Louie broke the silence: "I'm going to sit in the living room for a minute."

"You do that," Charlotte said. She and Inez decided to start packing up the kitchen, at the front of the apartment. Since the kitchen was the typical long, narrow Manhattan kind, in which three people could hardly maneuver at once, I said I would begin going through the things in Aunt Selma's bedroom. I passed Uncle Louie sitting on the small fold-out couch in the living room, staring in the direction of the silent television. The couch, upholstered in a gray and pink abstract print involving different sized rectangles, must have been from the 1950s. Like everything else in the apartment, it was beautifully maintained. The other furniture in the room included a bookcase, two end tables holding a matching pair of lamps, and two small armchairs. A drop leaf table stood against one wall. Aunt Selma used to pull it out and extend it to use as a dining room table when she had guests.

"Are you all right?" I asked Uncle Louie.

"What? Oh, yeah," he said, turning to face me. "I'm fine."

"You look like something's bugging you."

"No, nothing's bugging me. Is something bugging you?"

"Me? No," I answered.

I proceeded to the little bedroom at the back. As always, it was exquisitely tidy. Dust wouldn't dare settle in Aunt Selma's absence. From the far wall, the bed jutted out between a pair of windows framed with sheer white curtains. Next to it stood a round night table with a glass lamp and a clock on a cream-colored, crocheted doily. The door to the closet in the corner was open, and I could see three clear plastic garment bags hanging neatly side by side, each containing a few articles of clothing: dresses, slacks, blouses, two jackets, arranged by category. A metal shoe rack on the closet floor held several pairs of stylish walking shoes, including one in cordovan leather with dark brown piping that I particularly liked.

Alongside the closet was a bookcase with three shelves that contained a sewing basket, various mementos, such as an oval glass paperweight with the inscription, "Atlantic City," and a little statuette of a nurse in a cap and cape. There was a collection of photographs of various relatives that included Inez and Stuart's wedding portrait, a picture of Charlotte holding Charles, Peter's college graduation picture, one of Aunt Selma and me at my medical school graduation, and a snapshot of Brad and me taken at the Jersey shore. Of the remaining pictures I decided on the spot to keep one of my father in a soldier's uniform standing with my grandparents in front of their house in New Brunswick and the wedding picture of my parents. It wasn't surprising that of all the Sternbergs, my parents were so well-represented in Aunt Selma's private gallery. She and my father had had a particular bond since she had lived with my father's parents, her brother and sister-in-law, for several years when he was a boy, before she attended nursing school.

There was one more framed photograph in the room, the portrait of Aunt Selma's parents, my great-grandparents. It stood alone, centered on the top of the shiny, mahogany dresser that took up most of the wall across from the bed. A dark-toned picture, the plain frame around it made it look even darker. The two stiff figures were seated side by side, glaring at the camera with expressions that could only be called menacing. My great-grandfather wore a fez, and my great-grandmother had an object resembling a dead bird, about the size of a crow, on her head. I wondered, as I always did when I looked at this picture, whether something was seriously wrong with them. Next to the photograph was a black, shellacked jewelry box etched with red and gold butterflies, and next to that, a matching tortoiseshell comb and brush.

Then I saw it. Sticking out from under the jewelry box, barely visible, was the corner of a scrap of paper. I lifted the jewelry box and found a newspaper clipping and a neatly folded 8 1/2 x 11 lined sheet covered with Aunt Selma's precise penmanship. The clipping was an obituary of one Harris Townsend, MD, dated three months before. I sat down on Aunt Selma's bed as I read it. He was 77 years old, had served in the Air Force in WWII, had been on the faculty at Lafayette in the department of anesthesiology for 34 years before retiring, etc., etc., survived by his wife of 52 years, the former Ida Loomis. He had died at Lafayette Medical Center of complications of surgery.

My fingers shook as I unfolded the other paper. It was a list of names that read as follows:

Dr. Divine
Shorty
Clark Gable
Goldilocks
Popeye
Nightingale
Betty Grable
Madame Curie

Shorty and Popeye had checkmarks beside them. My heart was speeding, and I thought: I'm going to bleed into my head.

There was a soft groan and footsteps, and instinctively I shoved the pieces of paper into my pocket. Uncle Louie appeared in the doorway and said, "How are you doing?"

"OK," I answered.

"You know, there are some books in the living room that you might be interested in. You ought to look them over."

"OK."

"What have you done so far?" He had stepped into the bedroom, and I suppose it looked like I hadn't done anything except sit on the bed.

"I'm just taking an inventory, you know, mentally" I said, ridiculously.

"Are you looking for something in particular?"

"Like what?" I asked.

He let out a short, staccato laugh, like a cough. "I don't know.

Nothing." He waved his hand as if erasing his words. "Just pick up everything and put it in a box."

"Well, you obviously haven't been doing that. You looked at the books."

He regarded me warily. "What have you found?"

"Nothing," I said. "What are you looking for?"

"*I'm* not looking for anything."

"Neither am I."

"I didn't say you were."

I glared at him and thought that, considering the plentitude of secrets in our family, not excepting an entire secret person in New Haven, one could be forgiven for looking around a little.

Uncle Louie turned toward the door. "I wasn't actually coming in here," he said. I sat still, listening to his footsteps as he walked toward the bathroom at the end of the hallway. When I heard the door shut, I slipped out to the kitchen with the obituary and list of names burning a hole in my pocket. Inez and Charlotte were seated on the floor, wrapping plates in newspaper and packing them in a box.

"Inez, can I show you something?" I asked, aware that my voice was at least an octave too high. Charlotte stared at me. Inez stood up and followed me to Aunt Selma's bedroom. I wanted to close the door, but that would have been the same as inviting Uncle Louie to join us. "Look at this," I whispered, handing her the two pieces of paper. "They were hidden under her jewelry box."

Inez was still reading the obituary when I heard Uncle Louie's footsteps in the hall again. I swept the papers out of her hands and returned them to my pocket. Stepping to the dresser, I lifted the top of the jewelry box and said, "So what do you think we should do with the jewelry?" Inez looked puzzled.

Uncle Louie stopped in the doorway again and asked Inez, "Did you get tired of the kitchen?" I began to lift pieces of jewelry out of the box and scrutinize them.

"No," she said. "Ma's in there. Nora wanted me to go through Aunt Selma's jewelry with her." Uncle Louie nodded, though I thought he gave me a fishy look.

Once he was gone, Inez mouthed the words, "What's going on?"

"Finish reading," I whispered, giving her the slips of paper again. I stood at her elbow and tried vainly to gauge her reaction as she read. Inez would have been brilliant at poker if she had played. Our generation didn't, though our parents had been devotees. I recalled standing at my mother's side watching my parents' and uncles' and aunts' frequent poker games when I was a child. They played at our dining room table, expanded with extra leaves, a roomful of deadpan Sternbergs and their handicapped emoting spouses. You would have thought a Sternberg would always win with that advantage, but then you wouldn't have known my mother, who could laugh and complain about her hand and wipe them all out. Her victories were particularly sweet because she gave her winnings, a pile of change, to me.

Inez finished the obituary, looked over the list of names, then whispered, "She wrote this list."

"You bet." I started pacing back and forth between the mahogany dresser and the window.

She reread the obituary, then the list.

"Do you think this Townsend was either Shorty or Popeye?" she asked.

"Whichever one he was, maybe Stanley's urologist was the other one."

"Stanley's urologist? What do you mean?" she said.

"Remember, when we were in the car—"

"Nora, please don't pace," she interrupted me.

I stopped abruptly. "Coming from the cemetery?"

"Yeah," she mumbled.

I waited as she continued to study the obituary and the list. "So a couple of old doctors died after surgery," she said.

"And an old nurse."

Inez sat down on the bed, and I took the papers from her.

"Of course," she said slowly, "very old people die. There's nothing unusual about that."

"Right."

"But you're implying that this list and the checkmarks make it seem…"

"Sinister?" I suggested.

She nodded. Interestingly, while I felt invigorated by my discovery, it seemed to deflate Inez. She sat hunched forward, examining her hands, now folded in her lap. She too had the essential Sternberg features, the thick black hair, in her case, cut short, the high cheekbones and mustard colored skin, and the height. This last trait was the one I was missing, and of course the only one I cared about. Her clothes were perfect, and her shoes always looked like she was wearing them for the first time. That was a Sternberg thing, too. We might be stiff-necked, we might be psycho, but we knew how to dress.

I sat down on the bed next to her and said, "You know, it's bothered me a lot that Aunt Selma was so agitated in the emergency room. Everyone chalked it up to delirium, but she was never confused. In fact, she was very lucid."

"So now you're wondering if she knew something was going to happen to her."

"Well, that's the thing. It was all about being at Lafayette. She kept saying she would die if she stayed there. She wanted to go to another hospital."

Inez started flicking her bangs around. "Is it possible that there's some, I don't know, some horrible medical malfunction. . . going on at the hospital that she knew about?"

"And that I don't know about? I don't see how."

We were both quiet for a minute, then, speaking under her breath, Inez said, "You know she was eccentric." When I didn't respond she continued, "Remember Zoltan?"

"Oh, please," I groaned. Inez shrugged.

"Zollie Bacsi," I whispered, Hungarian for "Uncle Zollie." We had been taught to use the Hungarian forms of address when referring to any aunt or uncle, or older cousin for that matter, who had died in Europe. The immigrant Sternbergs preferred the English terms, and our parents' generation preferred we dispense with "aunt" and "uncle" totally and use only their first names.

"I don't want to think about it," I said.

"Of course not. Neither do I. It doesn't mean it didn't happen."

"I know," I sighed.

This was a topic that Inez and I scarcely ever discussed. Zoltan was a pigeon, probably a number of pigeons, whom Aunt Selma believed to be the embodiment of her deceased uncle. She left tidbits of foods that he had enjoyed while in his human manifestation, such as palacsinta, the Hungarian version of crêpes, on the windowsill, and he visited frequently to dine. Inez disapproved of Aunt Selma's relationship with the pigeon because of its implications about her mental health, and I agreed, of course, but I was also afraid she might contract a disease.

"OK," I conceded.

"So maybe these were nicknames of old friends, and she was keeping track of their deaths. Don't elderly people read the obituaries all the time?"

"Then why was she so afraid of being at Lafayette?"

"Well, the only other explanation is that someone is going around the hospital murdering retired doctors and nurses, and she knew it," she said briskly, standing up.

"It does sound absurd when you put it that way," I said, following her out of the bedroom. Inez returned to the kitchen, and I lingered in the hallway a minute, then went back to the bedroom and stood surveying the furniture and closet. I wondered if there were other pictures of Aunt Bunny somewhere. I guessed that there were, and I wanted to find them. We had left the empty boxes and bags by the front door, so I retraced my steps down the hallway to fetch a few to start packing. As I passed the entrance to the kitchen I glanced at Inez and Charlotte emptying drawers of utensils. In the living room Uncle Louie was disassembling a pair of lamps. These were legitimate, honorable tasks, as was packing away the bedroom. Searching for something I had never been intended to see, however, was traitorous. Worse than that, I didn't find it. I considered looking in the living room, although that seemed a less likely place to hide something. Anyway, snooping around with Uncle Louie beside me was out of the question. I realized I might have to be content, for the time being at least, with the one photograph I had.

I didn't know about Inez, but I was thoroughly distracted for the rest of the day. We worked until late afternoon, stopping only to eat a lunch of leftovers from the *shiva* that Uncle Louie and Charlotte had packed up. "The funeral baked meats did coldly furnish forth the emptying of the apartment," I quipped, chewing on a whitefish sandwich. No one thought this was amusing.

By the end of the day, we had managed to sort through the entire contents of Aunt Selma's apartment and pack a great deal of it into boxes to be hauled away. A less repressed family might have had a harder time of it and taken longer, but we soldiered on, unencumbered by the necessity of expressing our emotions. Uncle Louie went through the books with the rest of us, to see if anyone wanted anything in particular. There was an old set of Encyclopedia Britannica, some hardbound Reader's Digest compilations, a biography of John F. Kennedy, the 1945 edition of *Grant's Atlas of Anatomy*, a thin, weathered red leather-bound book titled, *The Nurse's Journey*, and a few other volumes. I took the anatomy text and the nurse's book.

That night I was physically exhausted but still dwelling on the obituary and list of names. I lay awake in bed, reading the list over and over. I had memorized the names long before Brad called. He agreed with Inez that we should interpret the findings as just another example of Aunt Selma's foibles. But I was unconvinced. Brad was biased by how peculiar he found the Sternbergs to be. And neither he nor Inez had been in the emergency department with her. They hadn't failed to save her life.

Although I usually fall asleep instantly, a residual effect of residency, I couldn't cork off. I went into the kitchen for a drink of water and sipped it as I leaned against the doorway to the living room. Grant's heavy, yellowed textbook and *The Nurse's Journey* lay on the coffee table where I had dropped them earlier. I wondered what the nurse's story was about. I had noticed it before on Aunt Selma's bookshelf, and she had told me it was given to her when she graduated nursing school. I picked it up and opened to the first page.

Penned on the inside cover, in an angular hand, was the following inscription:

To Selma M. Sternberg, R.N.,
We are so proud of you!
Your loving sister,
B

I hugged the book to my chest, because I thought my heart would break.

CHAPTER FIVE

Jessica found the existence of the obituary clipping and list of names fascinating. She was even willing to consider the possibility that it put Aunt Selma's agitation in a different light. I told her about Inez's and Brad's concordant interpretations, while we ate lunch in the atrium.

"You know," I sighed, "I wish, in retrospect, that we had asked for an autopsy."

"Well, you know you still can," Jessica said slowly.

"No, I can't, actually. The person who would have to give consent is my Uncle Louie, my aunt's brother, and I can't imagine even discussing it with him."

"Maybe you should try," she said in a gentle voice.

"No," I shook my head. "Out of the question." I took a sip of coffee. "I wonder if the hospital's aware of the three deaths, I mean, if anyone's connected them?"

"Three?" Jessica asked. I told her about the urologist.

"There's the person to ask," she said, nodding in the direction of the coffee shop exit. Stepping out with his lunch on a tray was Martin Baxter, a tall, blond-haired, green-eyed, unusually handsome invasive cardiologist in his early forties. His attractiveness had lately been marred, however, by an unfortunate tic he had developed since becoming chairman of the Medical Center's Quality and Untoward Event and Loss Limitation Committee (QUELL).

"Isn't that Michael Carter walking behind Martin?" Jessica asked.

I nodded.

"Have you spoken to him since right after your aunt died?"

"No," I said. "When I ran into him the next morning, here, actually, just after talking to you, it was so awkward. I mean, what can either of us say?"

"I guess you're right," she said.

Martin spotted Jessica's hand in the air and threaded his way toward us through the crowded atrium.

"I'm sure he won't want to talk about this at lunch," I said.

"Tough," she replied, swallowing. "It's part of his job."

We smiled innocently at Martin as he claimed an empty chair from an adjacent table and swung it around to join us. He was wearing hospital scrubs and clogs, having come straight from the cardiac catheterization lab. I was reminded of the advice given to me by a brilliant woman resident I had as an intern, never to trust a man in clogs. Martin greeted us energetically as he opened a carton of skim milk. I couldn't help but notice that the short sleeves of his scrubs revealed long, muscular arms covered with blond hairs that were visible when the light filtering into the atrium hit them just right. His arms pivoted hypnotically as he began to eat his yogurt. Over his shoulder I was vaguely aware of a table of female medical students watching us. Martin was asking me something. Wrenching my attention from his chest and upper extremities, I looked at his face and shuddered. He had an unnerving way of leaning forward and staring intently into one's eyes when he spoke. This had been more dangerous before the onset of the tic. He asked me if we were very busy in PCIMC, and I told him I had been out for about a week because of the flu and my aunt's death. He murmured condolences.

Jessica politely gave him time to eat, then got to the point.

"Has anyone talked to you about a patient dying recently after elective surgery?" She asked. "Three patients, actually."

Immediately Martin's left periorbital muscles started to twitch. "No, I-I-I haven't heard anything," he stammered.

"I thought there'd be an incident report, at least, if not a request for a morbidity and mortality conference," she continued.

He coughed violently, and we had to wait while he controlled himself enough to speak. "I'm," he cleared his throat, "I'm pretty sure I haven't received anything." The left side of his face launched into fasciculations again. "Though I've been so busy with the N-N-N-" he took a deep breath and, with disproportionate force, not unlike a patient with Tourrette's syndrome, blurted out, "N-NATCH survey!"

He was referring to the biennial hospital inspection conducted by the National Accreditation of Tertiary and Community Hospitals commission, scheduled for September. The Medical

Center's reputation, and a sizable chunk of its funding, depended on renewal of accreditation. Every two years the commission inhabited the hospital for five days with license to open any closet, drawer, or medical record it chose, conducting the exhaustive inspection euphemistically called a survey. Since Martin's committee was charged with monitoring clinical quality issues, it was at the forefront of NATCH survey preparations.

"Well, then maybe we should write up some incident reports," Jessica said, turning to me.

Martin had hazarded a sip of milk, and now started to choke.

"Do you want to hear the gist of it?" I asked him.

He shook his head and managed to form the words, "Not now."

"Then I'll just write something brief and send it to you," I offered, trying not to embarrass him any further. It was a mystery to me why Martin had ever taken on a headache like the chairmanship of QUELL. This was a topic Jessica, Celine, and I had previously discussed. We concluded that he had done it as part of a larger plan to advance an academic career, not appreciating how toxic it would be. I had no doubt he preferred the relative simplicity of invading people's chests.

"How are the NATCH preparations going, Martin?" I asked to change the subject, instantly realizing my blunder. But Martin staunchly answered that everything was moving forward, which I supposed was his standard reply. Then he asked Jessica if she would put a discussion of the missing narcotics on the next medical staff meeting agenda. He managed to pronounce the word "missing" with only a minor twitch. I had no idea what they were talking about. Jessica explained that three vials of morphine and one of Dilaudid were missing from the medication room on Schilling Five.

"Missing?"

"Can't be found. Not there. Gone," she said.

"Wow."

Martin had finished his yogurt and seemed eager to leave. As he stood up, he asked if we were going to Griffin Garrett's dinner, and if we knew that a chair was being endowed in Garrett's name at the medical school. Jessica said she would attend, and I said I was undecided, which wasn't entirely accurate. I had no intention of going. "It'll be quite a bash," Martin predicted and with that he picked up his tray and said, very generously, I thought, that it had been nice chatting with us.

When he was a safe distance away, Jessica said, "Do you think he would have told me to put something on the agenda like that if I were a man?"

"What are you talking about?" I said.

"Everyone knows the procedure. You give whatever you want on the agenda to Mrs. Toth." Mrs. Toth was secretary to Bill Shell, chief of the medical staff, and scribe and keeper of the agenda for medical staff meetings.

"Maybe he forgot the procedure," I said.

Jessica allowed that he looked jumpy. "What are you going to put in writing to him?" she asked.

"Nothing," I replied. "I just wanted to end the discussion. How would I write it up, anyway?'"

"Your aunt's case is ambiguous," she said, "because it was a big operation. But dying after arthroscopy? Come on, didn't anyone think that was unusual?"

"I'd like to know what kind of surgery Townsend had."

"We could pull his chart," she shrugged.

"What happens to charts after people die?" I asked. Neither of us knew exactly. "They must get archived somewhere," I said, "though after some period of time, the hospital must have to destroy them."

"And bury the errors of yesteryear forever," Jessica said.

It was close to one o'clock and we had to get going, Jessica to endocrine consult rounds, and I to Schilling Three, where I was attending on the teaching service. As we left the atrium I asked what else she knew about the missing narcotics.

"There's not much more," she said. "Obviously someone took them. The lock on the narcotics box wasn't forced, so he or she used the key. All the nurses from every shift have been interviewed, and no one was aware that the key was ever missing." The discovery had occurred the previous week. "Can you imagine," she asked rhetorically, "so close to the NATCH survey? It's just the kind of colossal screw-up that would make us lose our accreditation."

The idea of the mighty Lafayette Medical Center losing its accreditation was terrible, but also a tiny bit thrilling. Of course, being out of a job and associated with wreckage would not be thrilling.

Jessica looked worried. "You *are* going to Griffin Garrett's dinner, aren't you?"

"Nope," I said.

"Why not?"

"Because I can't stand Griffin Garrett."

"No one can," she said. "But I have to go, and Ray and I won't have anyone to sit with." She was referring to her husband, Ray Forester, a pulmonologist.

"What about Celine?" I asked.

"She said she's planning on having sciatica." Celine had a herniated disc, and periodically suffered incapacitating lower back pain.

"I'm sorry, Jessica," I sighed, "but I can't go. I was 'Garroted' one too many times." That had been our expression during residency for interacting with Dr. Garrett. Usually the garroting victim was the resident covering the Emergency Department when Dr. Garrett was on call for Neurosurgery, something he continued to do into his seventies. I could still become instantly nauseated and diaphoretic recalling the experience of presenting a case to him and being minutely, aggressively questioned and humiliated. "Anyway, Brad will be in Hong Kong," I said.

Jessica said all the more reason to join her and Ray.

"And don't forget the medical staff meeting," she called as I beat it toward the elevator. "Your attendance record stinks."

CHAPTER SIX

Celine had a problem she didn't know about. I wished I didn't know about it, either, but for me the knowledge was inescapable. Celine's husband Frank, a pediatric cardiologist, had a girlfriend, and not just any girlfriend. She was Dr. Roberta Garrett, director of the anatomic pathology laboratory, wife of Dr. Phillip Toste, the pulmonologist, and daughter of Dr. Griffin Garrett. I was aware of this distressing liaison because Frank told me about it. He cornered me in the doctors' lounge, and after checking the cloak room, the men's room, and knocking on the door to the ladies' room to make sure we were alone, he blurted out his secret. Frank was even-tempered by nature, and not used to blurting things out. He stood very close, stooping over me, and I noticed his conjunctivae were bloodshot. A two-centimeter laceration crossed his chin, probably the result of a shaving accident.

"I can't tell you how guilty I feel," he said, "but I'm irresistibly attracted to her." I could imagine that someone might find Roberta

Garrett attractive, the way chrome is attractive. I was surprised that that appealed to Frank.

"You have to promise me you won't tell Celine," he pleaded.

"Tell Celine? Are you kidding?" I said. The last thing I wanted to do was get between the two of them.

Frank and I had been good friends since college. We had even gone out together a few times. I had introduced him to Celine during our residency and stayed friends with both of them. In college, Frank's black hair was already starting to gray, but I could see up close that the process was hastening.

"Frank, how could you?" I said. He looked like he might start to cry, and I thought fleetingly that pediatricians were definitely the most sensitive doctors. A surgeon in his shoes would never have cried. An internist—fifty/fifty.

"What about Harmon and Ellison?" I asked, meaning Frank and Celine's twin daughters.

Frank wiped his eyes with the back of his hand. "I know I have to break it off," he said.

I could also imagine that telling Roberta Garrett something she didn't want to hear could be unpleasant. She was a lot like her father, at least in public, which was the only way I knew her: haughty, imperious, generally not smiling. The whole situation was nauseating.

"I feel so much better," Frank said, and put his hand on my shoulder. "I knew it would help to talk to you." He had such an earnest, engaging smile, it was impossible not to want to help him, but I felt I hardly deserved any credit. He checked his watch and said, "I have to run. I'm late for x-ray rounds." With that, he took off for the ballroom, as the radiology reading room was called, and I crawled back to Schilling Three.

I was nervous about talking to Celine after that, figuring I had the choice of betraying her if I didn't say anything and betraying Frank if I did. Normally this kind of information was something I might have shared with Jessica. But I decided it would be too awful for both of us to know about Frank's infidelity while Celine was in the dark, so I kept it to myself. Celine had phoned me when she heard about Aunt Selma, but of course at that point that was all we talked about.

The next time I saw her was the second week after Aunt Selma's death. I was rushing to get out of the hospital and catch a train to New Jersey, having been summoned to the law office of my cousin Scott Spencer for the reading of Aunt Selma's will. As I crossed the atrium, heading for the lobby, Celine happened to be coming out of the coffee shop. I glimpsed a helmet of straight red hair in my peripheral vision and was telling myself, absurdly, that it wasn't her and to keep moving, when she called my name. I came to a stop and she caught up with me.

In her characteristically dispassionate way, she said she had a problem she wanted to talk to me about. So, Celine had discovered it on her own and I would inevitably be trapped between the two of them. I noticed she was wearing earrings that didn't match. She and Frank were both falling apart.

"I'm sorry," I told her sincerely. "I'm running to catch a train to New Jersey."

"Is everything all right with your family?" One thing about Celine, she could always focus her attention on other people's dilemmas in a pinch. I guess that was handy for a psychiatrist.

"Yeah, thanks, just stuff," I said. I began to move backwards in the direction of the lobby and asked if I could call her at home in the evening.

"No, not at home," she gasped.

"Well, how about tomorrow, in the hospital?" I continued my regress toward the door.

She nodded and said, "Yeah, that's OK."

"Do you know your earrings don't match?"

"What? No," she said, pulling them off.

I left her studying her earrings in her palm and escaped through the lobby to the street, cutting it even closer for my train.

The most direct way downtown was the hospital shuttle that ran between the Medical Center and the Lafayette Midtown Eye Institute, an outpost of the Lafayette empire. From there I could walk the few blocks to Penn Station. The shuttle departed hourly from the circular drive in front of the main hospital entrance, where a line was already forming to wait for the next van. On the other side of the entrance a row of patients leaned or sat in wheelchairs configured along the hospital's sparkling granite façade, smoking cigarettes. Smokers had retreated outside in 1987, four years earlier, when Lafayette instituted its hospital-wide tobacco ban.

Most wore jackets over hospital gowns and a few had on their hospital-issue blue Styrofoam slippers. I looked to see if I recognized anyone from clinic. PCIMC patients, generally on Medicaid or uninsured, tended to be over-represented in the smoking line. Sure enough, I noticed Byron Davis, a patient of mine for the past few years. He looked in my direction and I waved.

"Hi, Doc," he greeted me. Wearing an unzipped army jacket, he was sitting in a wheelchair with a half-full Foley catheter bag dangling over the back. His left arm was pinned against the arm of the wheelchair, and with his right hand he was laboriously wiping the lenses of his eyeglasses with his hospital gown. I happened to know he was in his mid-fifties, though he looked twenty years older.

I moved closer and said, "I didn't know you were in the hospital."

"I've been here for three days," he said. "Had a stroke."

I winced and said, "I'm sorry."

"Yeah," he answered, his mouth drooping.

I asked him what floor he was on and he said seven, by which I assumed he meant Fishkin 7, the neurology service. After a long pause he said, "But I quit smoking."

"So what are you doing here?"

"Just breathing the air. I couldn't go cold turkey." He produced a hemiplegic version of a wry smile.

I wondered if he had been rationing his antihypertensive medication, as he had done in the past, to stretch it out. His problem was an absence of medical insurance complicating a chronic deficiency of money. These were poor prognostic indicators. He didn't qualify for Medicaid because he owned a pick-up truck. But to understand the brilliance of his circumstances, it was necessary to know that he supported himself, up until now, with a small handyman business that he ran out of the truck.

"I haven't seen you in clinic in awhile," I said.

"Well, I figured I'd wait 'til I had some money to buy my pills."

I could have gotten him free samples of medicine from the limited and erratic supply that the pharmaceutical companies pushed in PCIMC to get doctors hooked like heroin addicts. None of our uninsured clinic patients could afford to buy the drugs when their free supply ran out and was replaced by something new and different. So operating on the principle that something was better than nothing, we used what we had, and welcomed the pharmaceutical detailmen and women into our clinic over and over to drop off their goods. However, Mr. Davis knew about that. The visits themselves cost plenty.

The hospital van pulled into the circular driveway. "Well, Mr. Davis, I'd like to see you in clinic after they let you out of the hospital," I said.

"I know. Thanks, Doc," he answered.

I turned to catch up with the line now surging toward the van. Poor Mr. Davis. Once he got a load of his hospital bill I wouldn't be seeing him much in clinic, I reckoned. I made a mental note to call him after he was discharged, assuming his telephone was still turned on.

Joining the shuttle line I landed on another planet. In front of me was Wally Todd, chief of the department of medicine, talking to a woman I didn't recognize. She had beautifully arranged blond hair, a camel overcoat, and a thin, elegant attaché case that hung from her shoulder on a narrow leather strap. I surmised she was either a wealthy donor—but then what would she be doing with Wally?—or a high-ranking hospital administrator. Not that Wally, dressed in an impeccable charcoal gray trenchcoat over a gray suit, looked out of place next to her. As he spoke he rocked almost imperceptibly back and forth on the soles of his shoes, straight as a ruler. No one was ever surprised to learn that Wally was the son of a diplomat in the Eisenhower administration and had attended high school in Switzerland. He, himself, was not overly endowed with diplomacy but was rather known for his mercurial temperment and readiness to chastise the junior faculty.

It appeared from their conversation that they were off to a meeting at the state-of-the-art ambulatory care building that the hospital was opening in midtown in the hope of attracting busy executives. The blonde woman's attaché jiggled as she spoke, and I could make out a few of the gold embossed letters on the clasp: "Sr. V. P." Wally was rattling on about clinical research opportunities, but the Sr. V. P. interrupted him.

"We have something on the agenda," she appeared to be reminding him, "that's *much sexier*."

Sexier? She gave her head a little toss as she said this, which from the dorsal view looked like she might be getting ready to seize.

I leaned in as close as I could without falling on top of them.

"You know what I'm talking about," she said, and made a throaty, gurgling kind of noise.

I looked from her to Wally and back. No way, I thought.

"I haven't heard the whole plan," Wally said somewhat stiffly.

"Of course you haven't. That's why we've invited you to this meeting."

Wally flinched.

"It's called the 'Chief Executive Option,'" she breathed, as if the words themselves were thrilling. "We'll provide ten-minute in-and-out check-ups in the new building for, you know, 'the busy corporate leader.' Plus house-calls in their offices, and, this is the biggest selling point, I think, around-the-clock direct beeper access to the executive's private physician." Her head started to bob again.

"Private physician?" Wally asked.

"Well, one of our employees, of course."

Wally gritted his teeth. "One of our *physicians*," he corrected her, but she was oblivious.

"The company, whatever it is," she continued, "would pay an annual fee to cover the costs for each member enrolled in the plan."

"They may not be willing."

She waved her hand dismissively and said, "Oh, I think they will." She went on to explain that if a corporation was too stingy to participate, a personal plan was available for any top dog who wished to pay out of pocket for the same services.

Wally managed to force a dyspeptic smile. I considered her proposition. Everything being relative, I supposed executive suites were sexier than the smoking line, though care of the sick in general struck me as an odd hunting ground for sexiness. Outside of the operating room, that is, where the doctor-nurse and even male-female doctor relationships always had a strong sexual undercurrent.

By this time we had surged to the door of the van, and I took a seat toward the front, nodding at Wally as I passed him though he was too engrossed in conversation to see me. I tried to imagine him selling the chief executive option to the doctors in our department. The problem was that unlike Ms. Sr. V. P., who was clearly hallucinating, Wally, if ordered to do so, would try to make it real. I wondered how much money the hospital could make on a project like this. How much of it would go to the executive's physician, beeper at the ready 365 days a year, and would there be any dregs left at the bottom for lowly PCIMC?

I was on the sunny side of the van. As it plodded down Columbus Avenue in afternoon traffic, I grew sleepy. Residency had trained me, among other things, to take a nap anywhere, any time. Off-Broadway theaters were more comfortable than Broadway, I had found, because the seats tended to be a little roomier. Brad put up with this, as long as I was discreet. People working in the theater in the last decades of the twentieth century were like Medieval monks, anyway, he believed, maintaining it on life support until the arrival of a more enlightened time.

I woke up with a jolt in front of the Eye Institute and had to scramble to Penn Station, weaving through the pedestrian traffic, to make the 2:17 to Metuchen, New Jersey. At that hour the station was relatively uncrowded, and I probably could have bought my ticket at the ticket counter, but I didn't want to chance it. I raced through the waiting room, glancing at the departures board, and down the long flight of stairs to the loud, clanging track level. Here the sun didn't penetrate, and everything was lit with a deathly greenish glow. The staircase terminated on a platform between two tracks, upon each of which a train waited with its doors open. A trainman in a black uniform and cap, wearing eyeglasses with lenses as thick as the bottoms of soda bottles, approached me, limping slightly. "Metuchen?" I asked, and he inclined his head a quarter of an inch toward the train on the right. I boarded the nearest car, practically empty, and quickly found a window seat.

The train rolled, then wrenched forward and rocked along the track in the pitch dark tunnel. "Tick-ets!" the conductor's voice preceded him as he advanced through the cars. I had to empty every stray coin out of my pocketbook to come up with enough cash for the ticket and the surcharge for buying it on the train. I knew if I couldn't pay him the conductor would throw me off the train and I'd have to wander the tracks under the Hudson River forever.

Within minutes the train burst out of the tunnel onto the flatlands of northeastern New Jersey. As it rolled through the marshes and the steady succession of decayed cities, I was able to watch unimpeded the passage of the industrial wasteland that was so familiar I had to admit I loved it. Not admired it or approved of it, just loved it. From the angle of the grimy train window as we passed over a low-lying railroad bridge, I viewed the place where the turnpike rises and arches high over the marsh. As a child I had looked at the same scenery from the back of my parents' car when we drove to and from New

York on a Sunday to visit Aunt Selma, something we did frequently. I loved everything about those visits: the ride up quiet Manhattan streets, which were nearly empty on Sunday mornings, the smell of the landing outside Aunt Selma's apartment, the thick little brown enameled cups filled with chocolate pudding that she kept in the refrigerator and which she served with an inch of heavy cream poured on top. If the weather was nice we would all take a walk up one side of Seventy-second Street and down the other. Sometimes we ducked into Norwood's, the bakery whose butter cookies my mother was fond of, and bought some to bring home. When it was time to leave, Aunt Selma would accompany us to the lobby and stand in the glass doorway saying "So long" and waving at us. I used to walk backwards, repeating "So long" and waving, until the lobby receded from view.

On the highway we soared over the marshes, and their sprawl of junk was distant and impersonal. But on the train I sat eye to eye with the corroded walls of old factories and freight cars rusting in rail yards interspersed between the stations. I always enjoyed seeing the big Fait Tout Steel company sign, asserting its culturedness among the boxcars and scrap metal as if it were the most natural thing in the world.

We arrived at the Metuchen station right on time. A blast of icy wind scorched my face as I stepped onto the platform. I crossed under the tracks and walked a couple of blocks south on Main Street, past the post office, to a row of well-kept old houses that had long ago been transformed into offices. Scott's office was in the second house. Just as I turned onto the paved walk leading to the front porch, Uncle Louie and Inez rounded the corner of the building from the parking lot. Charlotte followed, pushing Charles in his stroller. He was embedded in layers of wool and cotton—Inez clothed him exclusively in natural fibers, even though the seventies were over— and, as I squatted beside the stroller, I was amazed at how much his round frowning face resembled a disapproving Sternberg. Charlotte, knowing I had come directly from the hospital and was therefore likely to be coated with micro-organisms, observed me warily. With the exception of Aunt Selma, and I suppose, myself, the Sternbergs practiced an antiseptic pre-penicillin-era vigilance against germs. It bordered on phobic. I was tempted to declaim that I had washed my hands after seeing my last patient. Not wanting to rattle her, however, I said nothing and was careful not to get too close to the baby.

Inez had taken command, as usual, and delegated the supervision of Charles to her mother. "We don't want to be late, Ma, we'll see you later," she said, and Charlotte and Charles embarked in the direction of Metuchen's attenuated downtown. Uncle Louie, Inez, and I proceeded across the porch into Scott's office. His secretary, who introduced herself as Lisa, directed us to an alcove where we hung our coats while she announced our arrival on an intercom.

Scott emerged from an inner chamber and led us to a conference room where he seated us at one end of a long, rectangular table. He was my second cousin and about ten years older than Inez and I. Not counting Aunt Selma's funeral, where I hadn't gotten a good look at him, I hadn't seen Scott for several years. I found him virtually unchanged. He had less of the Sternberg stamp than the rest of us, being fair-haired and even freckled, but he had apparently inherited that gene for growing older without putting on weight. In the interim he had acquired a nice office for himself, I thought, looking around at the bookshelves and framed art. Scott had always been shy and consequently a little brusque. Now he got right down to business and started reading the will.

"It's very straightforward," he began. That was hardly surprising.

"I, Selma Miriam Sternberg, residing at 300 West—" Scott's voice was momentarily subsumed by an explosion in my head. I shut my eyes, gripped the table edge and leaned forward so I'd have a shorter distance to fall. I'll be the first Sternberg to ever faint in public, I thought. On the other hand, did a small gathering of Sternbergs count as public? All I could see were purple blotches expanding and dissolving between my head and the floor, and I was afraid I might vomit. I laid my head on the table, which was cool to the touch, shut my eyes, and clapped my hand over my mouth, but nothing happened. Under the roar I could just perceive the sounds of a fluttering around me.

"Nora, are you all right?"

"Get down on the floor."

"Lisa, please bring in a glass of water."

The nausea subsided. "I'm OK," I said. They were all gawking at me.

"How did you know you're supposed to get down on the floor?" I said to Uncle Louie.

"Everybody knows that," he said.

"Have you ever fainted?" I asked him.

"No."

Of course he hadn't.

I sat upright in the chair and without realizing it, started taking my pulse at my wrist.

"You're taking your pulse," Uncle Louie observed.

"Oh, sorry," I said, and dropped my hand.

"Nora, should we wait a little bit?" Scott asked. He handed me the paper cup of water that Lisa had brought in.

"She hasn't gotten over the flu yet," Inez explained.

I assured them that I was fine.

Scott hesitated until I had finished my drink.

"Would you like a cup of tea?" his secretary asked me, standing in the doorway. "I can make you a cup of tea."

"No really, thanks, I'm fine."

"OK," Scott proceeded, "OK—you're sure?"

"Yes."

"OK. Where were we?" He leaned over the will on the table in front of him and resumed, "…make this will hereby revoking all previous wills and codicils. First: I appoint my brother, Louis Sandor Sternberg, presently residing in New Brunswick, New Jersey, as the Executor of this, my Last Will and Testament." Scott paused and looked across the table at Uncle Louie, who nodded vaguely and seemed to be preoccupied, though I couldn't imagine with what. The next few lines covered the contingency of Uncle Louie predeceasing Aunt Selma, or failing to qualify as executor, in which case the second candidate for executor was Scott. I wondered why not Aunt Tootsie. Maybe Aunt Selma had thought she was too far away.

Scott was reading on, "...my estate, real, personal or mixed, of whatsoever kind or nature, and wheresoever the same may be situate, of which I may die seized or possessed, or to which I may be entitled at the time of my death..." I marveled at the way attorneys could prepare for any number of competing outcomes. "...to my Trustee, Scott Spencer, residing in Metuchen, New Jersey, to hold and manage in Trust nevertheless, to be applied solely to the use of my sister, Bella Rebecca Sternberg, residing in New Haven, Connecticut, to pay all expenses incurred by her residence at Vista View Rest Home, or any other facility, domicile, or establishment in which she may from time to time reside, and to all other use of my said sister, taking into consideration her best interests and welfare, in such amounts as my Trustee, in his absolute and uncontrolled discretion, shall from time to time determine."

Not only that, it turned out Scott had previously been appointed Aunt Bunny's conservator for health care decisions, a fact I apparently hadn't needed to know.

There were a few more paragraphs detailing the ways the Trust could be invested, reinvested, consolidated, allocated, transferred, diversified, and so forth. And that was the will in its entirety, with the exception of one little bequest that I could never have anticipated. Scott cleared his throat before reading on.

"I hereby bequeath to my grand-niece, Inez Lillian Diamond, residing in Hoboken, New Jersey, my silver flower brooch." Scott stopped reading because he had come to the end. He looked around the table, waiting for us to react.

"What brooch?" Uncle Louie asked.

I knew exactly what brooch. It was Aunt Selma's most prized piece of jewelry, a silver pin in the shape of a curving stem, with two tiny sapphires making up the flower. She had worn it on every important occasion I could remember, and I had always admired it.

"Wha-what about Nora?" Inez stammered. Her face was flushed, and I could feel my own skin burning. Then she turned to me and said, speaking fast, "You take it, Nora, I don't want it."

"No, I won't take it," I said.

It was an awkward moment. "Usually families argue about what they want to claim, not give away," Scott proffered, trying to diffuse the tension.

No one acknowledged him. Uncle Louie, who had been sitting for some time with his arms folded across his chest, staring into his lap, suddenly looked up and said, "The girls will work it out." Then he rose, ending the conference.

We filed out of the conference room in silence, and Scott walked us to the front door. He waited while we gathered our coats and hats, which Inez and I managed to do without looking at each other. We thanked him, said goodbye, and stepped onto the porch to catch sight of Charlotte pushing Charles up and down the sidewalk. Charles was stuffing a chocolate bar in his mouth, holding it with both mittens. His fleece-covered legs, straight as boards, pumped up and down excitedly.

"Oh, not candy, Ma," Inez wailed, bearing down on the stroller.

"We ran out of those little things you gave me," Charlotte said.

"Those little things," Inez panted, trying vainly to unclamp

Charles' fists, "are organic, whole-grain, growth-hormone-free, fruit-juice-sweetened…cereal…pieces."

"Charlotte, if you want to say hello to Scotty you should do it so we can leave," Uncle Louie said as he descended the steps from the porch.

Charlotte hurried inside while Inez continued to struggle with Charles, who was now kicking and bellowing in rage. When she finally pried loose the candy, she grabbed the handlebars of the stroller and thrust it forward toward the parking lot. Charles sobbed, shuddering with fury and indignation. Uncle Louie and I followed and stood next to the car while Inez, declining our offers of assistance, unfastened Charles and pulled him out of his stroller. She maneuvered him into his car seat, and Uncle Louie stowed the stroller in the trunk. While Inez's head and thorax were thrust deep in the back seat, I said to Uncle Louie, "Why did you want me to come to this? I didn't have to be here."

"I didn't ask you to be here," he said.

"Yes, you did. You asked Inez to ask me."

He took a step back and let out his staccato blast of laughter. Then he said, "Only for the pleasure of your company. Although I really didn't ask Inez."

"Yes you did," I persisted. "She said so."

"She did? I don't remember. Well, did you want to be left out?"

That was an interesting question. "Maybe," I said.

"You're upset about Selma's brooch."

"Ha. Not in the least," I answered haughtily. I wasn't sure if he rolled his eyes, because he turned to get in the car.

Charlotte reappeared and they all climbed in, Inez behind the wheel. She backed the car out of its parking space, stuck her head out the window, and said, "Nora, I'll call you later." I nodded and waved to them as they turned down Main Street.

I headed in the opposite direction, retracing my steps on the sidewalk along Main Street, back to the train station. The next train to New York wasn't for another twenty-five minutes, so for no good reason, and certainly without any judgment, I set off on a stroll up Woodbridge Avenue. I passed the loading dock behind the post office and the new row of condominium townhouses that had been squeezed into the lot across from the station, and approached the side street on which stood my old elementary school. Hesitating at the top of the street, I suppressed my instinct to turn and run and stepped onto the neatly shoveled sidewalk. This was a wide street of vintage houses with front porches and detached garages that could have been on the cover of a magazine of Americana. It looked just like it had some twenty-odd years ago. Halfway down the street, to the left, was the short cul de sac leading to the school yard behind the old tan brick school building. I turned into the cul de sac, and before I had fully processed what I was doing, I was standing on an icy patch of cement behind my old school.

There was a wire fence along one side of the schoolyard where honeysuckle vines bloomed in the spring, and I went looking for it. To get there, I circled the perimeter of blacktop behind the school building, surprised at how small it was. This was the area where girls had played "double Dutch" at recess, calling out "D-I-F-S-G-J," short for Dutch, Italian, French, Spanish, German, and Japanese, each with its own particular jump rope step, but I couldn't remember what the boys did. After recess we had lined up here in fidgeting rows, waiting to be allowed back in the building. It was late afternoon now, almost dusk, and the schoolyard was deserted. The dirt field that stretched from the edge of the pavement to Woodbridge Avenue was still there, covered with snow and islands of frozen mud, but without a fence or vines. I wondered if I had dreamed them. I was sure I had remembered them more than once. Maybe I had dreamed them more than once, or remembered a dream repeatedly.

A loose chain whipped against the steel flagpole, and crumbling leaves flitted by my legs. Feeling like a trespasser, I hurried back across the schoolyard, to the street. This way was empty, too, and eerily quiet, except for a young mother walking with a chubby little girl in a snowsuit who skipped along beside her. The girl was counting as she skipped, and the mother held her mittened hand. As soon as I passed them I broke into a run, despite an aching pain in my chest. I cursed myself for indulging a stupid, sentimental urge. Served me right. I didn't stop until I crossed the threshold of the train station. I bought the *Times* from a vending machine and obliterated the crossword puzzle, keeping my head down all the way back to New York.

The moment I entered my apartment, before I could even hang up my coat, the phone started ringing. It was Inez, bursting to talk about Aunt Selma's unexpected legacy. Inez explained that she had been thinking about the will the whole way home from Metuchen and had concluded that it was just another example of how eccentric, how *odd*, Aunt Selma could be.

"Please don't worry about it, Inez," I said.

"I'm not worried, but it reminded me that she was capable of doing peculiar things, which made me think maybe the list you found in her bedroom doesn't mean much of anything, you know?"

So the list had made an impression on her. "Do you really think so?" I asked. Although I didn't say it to Inez, nothing would have put my mind at ease more than to believe Aunt Selma's death had been a bona fide post-operative complication.

Inez lowered her voice. "You know what I'm talking about."

"Oh please, Inez, not again." I didn't think I could stand another discussion about Uncle Zollie.

"I don't mean the pigeons," she said imperturbably. Her willingness to discuss Aunt Selma's delusions made me wonder if she had a stronger stomach than I. "Even if you think that the business about Uncle Zollie was just something fanciful—"

"Fanciful? Are you suggesting she didn't really mean it?"

"There were other things," she continued. "Do you think it's normal to hear people speaking to you when there's no one there?"

I didn't say anything.

"Isn't that considered psychotic?" she asked.

"What?"

"Hearing voices!"

"Oh. Well. It's more psychotic in some cultures than others," I said weakly.

"Uh-huh. All I'm saying is she was a little, you know, well, let's face it, she's not the only one."

I sank into the couch, still in my coat, holding the phone in my lap. My heart was pounding.

"So maybe she liked to make up nicknames for people," Inez speculated, "and she kept a list of old friends. That's not even nuts." Or maybe, she went on, there was some other perfectly innocuous, if unorthodox, explanation for the list of names. Likewise, Aunt Selma might have saved the doctor's obituary because she knew him. Perhaps she had worked with him. What was wrong with that? We should entertain the possibility that we had jumped to conclusions. (This was magnanimous of her; it was I who had jumped.) Aunt Selma had possessed a colorful personality, and what right did we have, after all, to invade the privacy of her dresser top and concoct some bizarre, nefarious explanation for what we found there?

I was worn out overall, and easily seduced by her reasoning. With mutual relief we continued in that vein until we had satisfied ourselves that we had invented everything. I hung up the phone happier than I had felt in weeks and within minutes was in my bed, sailing off to Nod.

I awoke when Brad phoned during a break in rehearsals, about 5:00 A. M. in New York, and recounted the events of the day. He had no opinion whatsoever about Aunt Selma's brooch. But when I told him how relieved I was to drop the idea that something pre-meditated had happened to her, he said he was just starting to believe it.

"Well, you're too late," I said.

"I was thinking you ought to find out if she told the ambulance driver to take her to the Medical Center or to a different hospital."

I sucked in my breath.

"Because," he continued, "if she told them to take her to Lafayette, then you'd know she saw something in the emergency room that made her think she was in some kind of danger."

"Everyone in the emergency room is in danger," I retorted.

"You know what I mean."

"Don't you think giving the brooch to Inez, and nothing to me, was a little weird?"

"I can't say anything about that," he said. "But it could mean there's a lot about her you don't know."

"It felt so good to give the whole thing up," I said.

"Then do it."

I asked him how *King Lear* was going. They were setting the play in an unnamed American city, where Lear, a retired advertising executive, was entering a nursing home after his first two daughters refuse to take him in.

"It's going very slowly," Brad sighed. "The Norwegians can't grasp the idea that someone would have to bankrupt himself in order to afford a nursing home. They think it's too contrived."

I fell back asleep and dreamed of a sad Viking king and a nursing home buffeted in a storm.

CHAPTER SEVEN

I was busy looking at a CAT scan in the ballroom when Celine paged me, and I used that, though not without guilt, as an excuse to postpone calling her back. Maybe she understood that I was trying to avoid her, because she didn't call again for the next several days. Meanwhile, I had resolved to stop worrying about Aunt Selma, and the quality of my life had improved considerably. February had arrived, my month to attend on the medical teaching service, as I was required to do once a year according to my contract with Lafayette. As a rule, the junior attendings get assigned to the in-patient service during the least desirable months, universally considered to be July and August, when the housestaff are new. But I learned that February can also be rough. The interns, having learned the ropes and passed their initial period of constant anxiety punctuated by brute fear, are now merely exhausted and starting to crack. By the time February rolls around, they've gone for weeks without seeing daylight while the hospital census runs high. For me, the long workdays and unending stream of admissions were, this time, helpful distractions.

On Friday morning of the first week, I arrived on Schilling Three a few minutes before eight o'clock, as usual, paper cup of coffee in hand. The floor was jammed with the customary traffic. Food service people pushed clanking metal carts, dispensing and collecting breakfast trays, filling the air with the smell of powdered scrambled eggs that is irreproducible outside a hospital, a nauseating smell. Two maintenance men stood on ladders next to the patients' lounge, hammering something into the ceiling. The day shift of nurses emerged from isolation after getting "report" from the night shift. Interns and residents crowded the nursing station, turning over charts and vying for telephones and computer terminals. A few private attendings flew past, scribbling in charts. I caught a glimpse of the two interns and the third- and fourth-year medical students on my team popping in and out of patients' rooms as they rushed to finish pre-rounding.

By the luck of the draw, I had been assigned to a team with an ace third-year resident, Paul Friend. At five minutes to eight he appeared, coming from morning report, the post-dawn ritual where residents and a handful of faculty attendings review admissions from the night before. Paul gathered up the charts strewn all over the nursing station and loaded them onto a mobile chart rack. He and the fourth-year student had been on call the night before, and, he informed me, had picked up three admissions and two transfers from the ICU in the last 16 hours.

"That's what we get for diuresing the service so well yesterday," he said, referring to our numerous discharges of the day before, making us sitting ducks for new admissions.

Paul steered the chart rack to the top of the north corridor. The interns and medical students joined us as our procession advanced to the door of the first admission. We parked several feet outside the door and stood in a little circle, and the fourth-year student, a tall, serious, soft-spoken girl named Tonya, began to present the case. Like a warm bath, the formulaic recitation—"An eighty-three year-old woman with diabetes and hypertension presented to the Emergency Department with four days of worsening shortness of breath and chest pain..."—washed over me. Tonya was well-organized and appeared to have rehearsed her presentation with Paul. The rest of us listened as the corridor buzzed with nurses, doctors, and even an occasional visitor at that early hour, such as the one who entered our patient's room. A few yards from us the nurses had positioned a small elderly woman, a geriatric waif, in an armchair at the edge of the hallway. Bent forward at the waist, she was secured to the chair by a restraint improvised from a hospital bed sheet. She had an unkempt plume of white hair and skeletal arms with which she beckoned to everyone who passed, shrieking, "Don't let them do it to me."

"Do what, Lillian?" one of the nurses leaned over the armchair and shouted at her.

"Oh," the woman said in a low voice, followed by an inaudible mumble.

I realized I was staring at her, and refocused my attention on the case presentation, which was now wending its way through the familiar, predetermined stages: the past medical history, the family history, the social history, the review of systems. By the time Tonya finished, it appeared that the patient, one Ms. Margaret Eichling, had actually done very well overnight. She hadn't succumbed to a heart attack, or a pulmonary embolism, or any of the other grisly items in the differential diagnosis. On the contrary, she had responded well to diuretics, and this morning she "looked like a rose," an expression that always made me nervous.

It was right about then, as the third-year student began, in accordance with tradition, to list the causes of congestive heart failure that the screaming started. Someone yelled, "Paul!" like she meant it, followed by "Call a code!" Paul was already sprinting into the room, with the two interns behind him. A nurse scrambled out of the room, grabbed the code cart from the hallway, and raced back in with it, yelling in the direction of the Nursing Station, "Call a code!" I had followed the interns, with the students behind me, and stood outside the half-circle formed around the patient's bed. Paul asked for Atropine and one of the nurses pulled the syringe out of the code cart. In the middle of it all was none other than our Ms. Eichling. The room was semi-private, and the patient in the other bed, the one nearer to the door, lay cowering with the sheet up to her chin. Then we heard the electronic siren, followed by the announcement, "code blue on Schilling Three North. Code blue on Schilling Three North." A nurse barreled through with an EKG machine, but Paul shook his head and started chest compressions, while one of the interns stood at the head of the bed and squeezed the Ambu bag.

The code team arrived and took over, but there was no bringing back Ms. Eichling. After a short while they packed it up, and the crowd that inevitably assembles during a code trickled away. I led our group to the nursing station to call Ms. Eichling's family, which, according to the face sheet in her chart, was a nephew in Pennsylvania. Paul made the phone call. As he spoke, I picked up a blank x-ray requisition on the counter and wrote on the back of it, "Ask for a post." Paul nodded, and after answering a sequence of questions, essentially repeating consecutively that he didn't know, he asked the nephew to consent to a post-mortem examination. He did it the right way, sensitively and reassuringly, and the nephew agreed.

When that was done, we trudged back to the chart rack, which had spun down the corridor in all the commotion. Naturally we wanted to stop what we were doing to perform our own post-mortem of Ms. Eichling's brief hospital course and react to her unexpected death. I gave us five minutes to talk about it, knowing that was hardly enough, but we had a big service to get through, and it would have to do for now.

We resumed rounds at the door in front of us. The first bed was occupied by a 64-year-old man with emphysema and cellulitis of his right leg. Roman, one of the interns, flipped through the index cards he carried in a stack, and said, "Mr. Crawley's on day three of amp and gent," using the resident abbreviations for ampicillin and gentamycin, "and the leg looks much better." We discussed his leg, his breathing, and his kidney function, then entered the room, assembling around the bed. The patient had a round, red face and sparse, matted gray hair and was propped up on two pillows, watching the little television set suspended directly overhead. Oxygen tubing was wrapped tightly around his neck, the nasal prongs sticking up against his cheek next to his nose.

"This won't do much good," Roman said, stepping forward and replacing the prongs in his nostrils. The patient surveyed us warily.

"How do you feel, Mr. Crawley?" I asked.

"All right," he answered, breaking into a spasm of coughing.

"May we look at your leg?"

He shrugged and stuck his right leg out from under the sheet. It was swollen and rock hard from the knee down, the skin a shiny violet, pocked and peeling and oozing clear fluid in places. Just above the ankle sat a glistening yellow ulcer, about the size of an egg.

"Much better," I said. Everyone nodded.

The leg was swiftly withdrawn.

"Was Vascular here?" I asked.

"Late yesterday," Roman said and added, in a louder voice than necessary, "You're going to start whirlpool treatments, Mr. C." The patient grimaced and resumed watching TV, clicking the remote control furiously. "I'll be back to see you later, Mr. C.," Roman said cheerfully.

We moved past the curtain to the next bed, only to find it empty and neatly made up. The third-year medical student, Patrick, told us that his patient had signed out AMA, that is, against medical advice, the night before.

We filed back to the hallway and took our positions around the chart rack. "What else do you want to say about that?" Paul asked.

Patrick looked at Michelle, the other intern, who said, "Florio didn't actually sign out, he eloped. Meaning no one took out his central line."

I sucked in air involuntarily. "Did he take the IV pole with him?"

Michelle cleared her throat. "No, but apparently he was seen carrying a little shopping bag. From Bloomingdale's," her voice trailed off.

"With the IV bag in it?"

"Apparently."

This was particularly problematic because Dale Florio, being treated for osteomyelitis, was an IV drug user. He had already survived several overdoses and multiple infections. It was inconceivable that he would be able to resist the lure of a direct conduit to his jugular vein.

"What did you do?" I asked Michelle.

Paul answered that since he had been the one on call the previous night, the nurses notified him when they discovered Florio decamped. "I called his house," he said, "and his girlfriend said she hadn't seen him. So I told her when she finds him she has to bring him back to the ER so we can at least get the line out."

"Who was it who saw him carrying a shopping bag?" I asked.

There was a silence, then Michelle said, "One of the other patients."

"Well that's just great. Another success."

We pushed the rack to the next door. As we walked, Tonya said sadly, "You know, Mrs. Eichling had been a nurse here. I mean, many years ago. She was a scrub nurse in the O.R."

"Excuse me?" I wheeled around to face her.

Tonya repeated, flustered, "She was a nurse here many years ago. I—I thought that was interesting."

It certainly was. I halted abruptly and demanded, "Who was the nurse who called the code, I mean who called for Paul, before they called the code?" They all looked at me, puzzled. "Remember? Someone yelled 'Paul!' " I continued, impatiently.

"Monique," Paul said.

"Right. Where's Monique?"

We flagged down the head nurse, wheeling a medication cart down the corridor, and she told us that Monique had gone on break.

"What exactly did you want to ask her, Dr. Sternberg?" Paul said. "Miss Eichling was unresponsive and bradycardic when I—"

"I know, Paul," I interrupted. "You told us. I want to know what happened before that."

"Before that? I don't think anyone knows."

"Did she have any history of bradycardia, of arrhythmia?" I demanded.

"No."

"Were her electrolytes normal?"

"Yes."

"Well, what medications had she gotten?"

It seemed for a moment that they were all watching me a little strangely. Of course we had already reviewed this. I realized I'd better get a grip, so I managed to say that we would see what the autopsy showed. Thank God for the autopsy, I thought.

We still had to pick up the pace, so we marched briskly through the remaining admissions, the ICU transfers, and the rest of the service. I struggled to stay focused. It took a huge effort to keep my mind off Margaret Eichling, and when we finally finished rounds I felt almost giddy. The housestaff and students were already a few minutes late for teaching rounds, their mid-morning conference, so they hurried off. The director of the residency program would chide me for keeping them late, but I would remind him that rounds were interrupted by a cardiac arrest. Normally at this time I would write my notes, which usually involved going back to see some of the patients again. Instead, I grabbed a phone at the nursing station and paged Jessica. She answered immediately, as opposed to promptly, which was her usual speed.

"Where are you?" I asked.

"In my office. I'm reading DEXAs," she said, meaning bone density studies. "You won't believe this. I did one on myself, and I have the bones of an eighty-year-old woman."

"Really? I have to talk to you about something," I said.

As I hurried to her office in the basement of the Tower Building, it occurred to me that I was hardly being discreet, and if someone was stalking old people at Lafayette, he or she might stalk right by me while I was on rounds or on the phone. I had barely finished that thought before I heard heavy breathing behind me and turned to find Leon Fabricant approaching at a rapid pace.

"May I talk with you while we walk?" he asked, though without his usual saccharine intonation. As we swerved along the corridors, he told me he had been talking to Martin Baxter, who had mentioned my observation about certain geriatric patients expiring in the hospital.

"Do you realize they were all my patients?" he asked. There was nothing remotely pleasant in his manner.

"No," I said.

"Well, they were." He stopped short, and to be congenial, I did too. "So if you have any concerns, I wish you would discuss them with me, rather than with Martin or whoever else you've been talking to."

"I spoke with Martin because he's the head of QUELL," I retorted. "Don't you want to find out what happened to your patients?"

"I know what happened to my patients," he snapped. "They were old and sick and they died."

"But two of them died after minor surgery." That was actually stretching it—I didn't know what surgery Townsend had had.

Leon's mouth dropped open, and he gawked at me, his face flushed. Above his immaculate white shirt collar his neck veins were distending in front of my eyes. He's becoming apoplectic, I thought. I was aware that people walking by were watching us. Leon worked his jaw a few times, succeeded in composing himself, and hissed, "Are you on QUELL?"

I shook my head.

"NATCH?" His voice was getting louder.

"No."

"Have you done any quality improvement work at all?"

"No."

"So you don't know what the hell you're talking about!" he shouted.

I answered, speaking very softly, and managing to keep my voice from quavering "I'm not convinced that my aunt died from complications of surgery."

He was momentarily speechless. Then he said, in practically a falsetto, "What do you think she died of?"

"I don't know."

He made a sharp, squeaking noise. Wiping his hand across his forehead, he blinked a few times, opened his mouth and closed it, and stood very still, reconstituting his oily veneer.

"Of course," he added calmly, "if there's any systemic problem I would want to be the first to know it."

I nodded, turned around, and continued down the hall without him. Well, I'll be sure to pass that on to Martin, I grumbled to myself. Other rejoinders occurred to me. I was moving so fast I almost broke into a run, but it wasn't necessary, Leon didn't try to catch up with me. I took a detour through the lobby to the atrium, for a cup of coffee to settle my nerves. Though I kept repeating in my head what a jerk he was, I was good and angry at myself for letting him bully me.

I picked up a cup of coffee for Jessica, too. Though she preferred it black, I added milk liberally in view of her bone age. She was sitting at her desk when I arrived in her office, which was a little larger than a very small closet. I sat in the only chair other than hers. Piled around us on the floor were stacks of journals and reprinted articles. There was a shelf of textbooks over her desk, and a tall filing cabinet against the wall next to the door. Jessica's desk was covered with mail and other papers, topmost being her DEXA reports, and her calendar, phone, and some framed pictures of Raymond and their children, Frieda and Drew.

I pushed the door closed and told her about my conversation with Fabricant, and the demise of Margaret Eichling, retired OR nurse.

"At least *she* wasn't his patient," she commented. "Why was she admitted to your service?" It was a legitimate question. My service was made up of patients from PCIMC, and any other patients admitted to medicine with Medicaid, plus/minus Medicare, or no insurance. A retired nurse would more likely have Medicare and some sort of private co-insurance, and the private doctor that came with it. She had had a private doctor in the community, come to think of it, someone who didn't have admitting privileges at the Medical Center. In cases like that, the patients were usually assigned to a Lafayette private attending from a list of names kept in the ER, according to a rotating system, rather than to the teaching service. The vernacular term for this process is "cherry picking."

"Let's see who was taking admissions last night," Jessica said. She picked up the phone, pushed the five digits for the emergency department, and asked the desk clerk who had been up for unassigned private admissions the night before. After a minute she thanked the clerk and hung up. "That's interesting," she said. "It was Leon."

"So he must have turned her down," I said.

She shrugged. "Guess so. But why are we talking about Leon, anyway? Do we suspect that he's bumping off patients?"

"I wouldn't want to say that."

"I mean, he's smarmy," she added, "but I don't think he's a bad doctor, necessarily."

"Why do you think he got so angry that I spoke to Martin?"

"He probably thought you were criticizing him."

"I didn't even know they were his patients! Except Aunt Selma." It really was quite a coincidence.

"Well, what do you think we should do?" Jessica asked.

"I don't know," I said. "Find every retired doctor and nurse in New York and warn them not to come to Lafayette. And certainly to stay away from Leon."

"Seriously, we probably should write an incident report for QUELL. Let them investigate it."

My beeper went off, flashing the Schilling Three extension. Jessica shook her phone free from the stacks of paper engulfing it and passed it to me. I dialed the extension and Paul answered.

"Hi, Dr. Sternberg. I'm sorry to tell you this, but Miss Eichling's nephew called me back and now he doesn't want the post."

"You're kidding," I groaned.

"No. Apparently his wife talked him out of it. I tried to change his mind, told him we didn't know exactly what happened to her, and we thought it was important to figure it out, that it wouldn't interfere with the undertaker's work, etc., but I couldn't convince him."

"Bummer."

"I know. I'm sorry."

"Don't worry. You did a good job."

I hung up the phone and returned it to Jessica. "No post on Ms. Eichling," I said glumly.

"Write something up about her death and give it to Martin," Jessica said. "She was doing great, and then, all of a sudden, she was coding. That's a reasonable thing for them to investigate."

"I guess so," I conceded. "Remember my aunt's list of names?"

She nodded.

"So who do you think Ms. Eichling was?"

Jessica didn't say anything.

"Maybe we should be calling the police," I persisted.

"And say what? 'Help! Old people are sick and dying in the hospital!'"

"Well, maybe they're not so sick. That's the point." I had to admit she was probably right, though, that we could only pursue it ourselves, which limited us to the clinical quality approach. And, like it or not, I was back on the case.

As I stood up to leave, Jessica said, "Do you want to hear the latest about the missing narcotics?"

"Oh sure, why not?"

"A bottle of morphine was stolen last night from Fishkin Four, right after a nurse who no one can identify asked another nurse for the narcotics key."

"And then what happened?"

"She went in the med room with the key, came out, gave the key back, and vanished. No trace of her. The next time one of the nurses on the floor opened the narcotics box it was short."

"But they must be able to describe her. No ID badge?"

"Not that anyone can remember. She was medium height, brown hair, lots of makeup. Had Latex gloves on."

"So at least we know she's not allergic to Latex," I said.

Jessica sighed, "That's about the speed of the investigation."

"The hospital's falling apart," I muttered.

"Did you get one of these?" Jessica asked, extracting a cream-colored engraved card from the piles on her desk and handing it to me. I nodded. It was an invitation from the Department of Neurosurgery to an afternoon reception at the hospital in honor of Griffin Garrett. "Apparently one party's not enough," Jessica said.

I opened the door. "Well, it's more than enough for me," I said, and headed back to Schilling Three.

CHAPTER EIGHT

I knew I would inevitably run into Celine and was feeling guilty that I hadn't returned her call, so it was with some element of relief that I finally encountered her, oddly enough, on the in-patient psychiatry unit.

I was finishing rounds with the Schilling Three team, trekking through the gyre of the Medical Center to Ten North, roughly a block away, where one of our patients was boarding. Ten North was the psychiatry floor, also known as the locked ward, and it was unprecedented for us to have a patient there. The poor patient was a thirty-eight year-old woman with schizophrenia and asthma, who had been admitted for a decompensation of the former and then developed an exacerbation of the latter. She wasn't ready to be discharged from the Psychiatry service, apparently still having abundant auditory hallucinations, but Ten North was unequipped to deal with a physically ill patient, so she had to be transferred to a Medicine floor. The only problem was that there were no empty beds.

So Michelle, who had been on call the night before, had worked up the patient on Ten North and been assured she would be transferred in the morning. By ten o'clock, as we were finishing rounds, the patient still hadn't moved.

Michelle rang the buzzer as we stood in the hallway outside the locked door. "They'll be happy to see us," she predicted. "The nurses have been calling me every thirty minutes all night."

"Yeah?" came a barely modulated voice over the intercom.

"It's Dr. Sternberg," I said.

The door buzzed open, although, I could have been anyone. It didn't matter, I suppose, since the purpose of the lock was to keep those inside from getting out.

Ten North looked like a regular ward that had been eviscerated, creating an empty central space where patients roamed chaotically. The nursing station was an enclosed booth with glass walls and fluorescent lights, accessed through a half-door, which was shut. Inside, several men and women in varying styles of dress sat crowded together without any identifying markers such as ID badges or uniforms. A few were writing in charts, others talking. Surrounding them were a chart rack, some overhead cabinets, and a desk occupied by the inanimate receptionist who had buzzed us in. Michelle let herself into the nursing station and grabbed our patient's chart. She was the only one of our team who appeared unfazed by the surroundings; she had already spent a significant amount of time there in the past twelve hours. It was an eyeful: patients milling around, pacing, rocking, some in hospital gowns, some in street clothes, and some in both hospital gowns and street clothes, some speaking, some silent. In the middle of the cavernous room, four sofas faced inward to form a square. A few patients sat motionless, staring fixedly ahead, and others circled the furniture, alternately sitting down and standing up.

I was reminded of my first experience on a locked ward as a third-year medical student. For my psychiatry rotation, I was assigned to a large psychiatric hospital in northern New Jersey. In those days smoking was still allowed in a few parts of the hospital, and everyone on the locked ward smoked all the time. I had barely set foot into the haze on my first day when a tall, burly man with a jagged beard stained yellow from nicotine strode to within an inch of my face, peered at my name tag, and thrust his hand in the air, exclaiming, "Heil Hitler!" Another man, shorter and stoop-shouldered, shuffled up to me, also stared at my name tag that identified me as a medical student, threw his head back and hollered, "The Chief Doctor has arrived!"

Our patient, Ms. Rhonda Goldfarb, was working on a nebulizer treatment when we reached her bedside. Fortunately, she was not in *extremis*. She was hearing voices that were sensibly commanding her to keep breathing. We stood outside the open doorway as Michelle presented the case. A bevy of curious patients gathered behind us, listening in, shaking their heads at frequent intervals and saying: "I have asthma, too" and; "That's a goddamn lie;" and "My rights are being violated" as Michelle spoke. A tall, emaciated man with a scraggly beard leaned over me, winking and whispering, "I'm the psychiatrist," as he pointed to his chest. Finally, much to my relief, a transporter showed up to escort Ms. Goldfarb on her long journey to Schilling Three. One of the Ten North nurses arrived to pack her up for the trip. I bolted into the room, pulled my stethoscope out of the pocket of my white coat, and asked the patient if I could listen to her breathe. She stared at me for a moment, then nodded slowly and put down the nebulizer mouthpiece. Paul slipped around to the other side of the bed, and we both listened, zig-zagging our stethoscopes across her back as she took a series of deep breaths. She was wheezing up a storm. I could see the nurse glaring at us from the foot of the bed, no doubt marveling that we had busted in to examine the patient just as they were about to expel her. I could see her point.

"I don't want to hold up the works," I told her sincerely, "but we've got to listen to her before she goes."

"I know," she sighed. She looked frazzled. "I just wish this had all happened earlier." Paul asked if she could check the oxygen saturation. She picked up the portable O2 saturation machine from the windowsill and, looking it up and down, said, "Let's see, I haven't done this since nursing school." Ms. Goldfarb glanced at her worriedly. She clipped the sensor to the patient's fingertip and in a few seconds the machine registered 97 percent.

"We're good to go," Paul said, smiling encouragingly at Ms. Goldfarb. He asked the nurse if the Schilling Three nurses knew they had to get a sitter, that is, someone to sit at the bedside and make sure our patient didn't elope.

The nurse was now attaching a miniature IV pole to the head of the stretcher. She nodded curtly and said, "They know." The transporter, who had remained somber-faced since his arrival, helped the nurse roll and pull the patient onto the stretcher. Meanwhile the nebulizer continued to rattle loudly and Ms. Goldfarb rhythmically puffed billows of mist, her gaze transfixed as if she were working on a hookah. As the stretcher pulled out of the room and headed across the ward, our audience of patients formed a parade behind it that grew as it approached the locked door.

Paul told Michelle to accompany the stretcher back to Schilling Three, and the rest of our team straggled behind, reviewing the interns' and medical students' lists of patients, to make sure we had rounded on everyone. "That's it," I said. "I'll see you all later."

"We'll look for you at noon conference, Dr. Sternberg," Paul said, leading the others toward the door.

As I passed the nursing station on my way out I heard a soft rapping on the glass. There was Celine, sitting next to the receptionist, talking on the phone and gesturing to me to come inside. I pushed open the half-door and tried to stand unobtrusively in a corner, waiting for her to hang up. More or less the same group of people I noticed earlier was still crammed in the nursing station. I was struck again by the array of costumes, and the absence of any clues as to job titles. How did the patients keep track of who was the doctor, the nurse, the social worker, etc.? As if they weren't contending with enough confusion to begin with. A lanky young man in light blue scrubs with slicked-back brown hair and aviator glasses said to the woman sitting next to him, "Darlene says she fractured a rib when she jumped off her night stand."

The woman, dressed in a pleated wool skirt and crewneck sweater with a demure gold necklace at the collar, sat writing in a chart propped in her lap. "Oh yeah?" she replied, without looking up.

"She says the x-ray showed a fracture."

"Who ordered an x-ray?" asked another woman, seated behind the first and also writing in a chart in her lap. This one wore a black skirt with a black tucked-in turtleneck and black tights. She had long blond hair and flame red lipstick.

"I don't know. I guess the Medical Consult," the man said.

Another man, older, wearing cuffed khaki pants, an Oxford shirt, and a navy blue blazer—an outfit commonly seen on non-surgical male doctors—leaned against the desk, also engrossed in a chart.

"Did the Medical Consult say there was a fracture?" the woman in the crewneck sweater asked.

"No. Darlene said so," the young man answered.

"Darlene's a patient," the older man said.

"Yes, I realize that."

"Well, you can't listen to patients," the woman in black tights said, looking up. "They're sick. They say things like, 'I'm God,' or 'I'm the Devil.'"

Celine hung up the phone and rubbed her face with the palm of her hand. "Unbelievable," she groaned to herself.

"What's wrong?" I asked. I was aware that everyone had stopped talking and was watching us. I'm getting paranoid, I thought. I'm turning into a psych patient just by being here.

Celine clasped her neck with both hands and rolled it from side to side. "The hospital bureaucracy is killing me." In the fluorescent light, she looked exhausted and pale, and I was suddenly incensed at Frank. Then she straightened her back and said, "What are you doing here?"

I told her about Rhonda Goldfarb.

"Oh, it's your service she's on. The whole unit's been freaking out." She stood up and said, "Come to my office. Do you have a few minutes?"

Her office was around the corner from Ten North, and I didn't have the heart to decline. When we got to the locked door Celine touched a button on the door, and we heard the receptionist's voice drone, "Yeah."

"It's Celine, can you let me out?"

The door buzzed, and we escaped. I followed Celine down the winding corridor and past the elevator bank to her office. A little rectangular plaque on the wall next to the door read, "Director of In-Patient Psychiatry." Celine unlocked the door with her key, doing it by touch, I imagined, in the dark hallway. Her office was more spacious than Jessica's tiny room in the basement, and even had a window, though it faced an airshaft. There was a desk of respectable size, three chairs, and a small sofa. The sofa had nothing to do with Celine's being a psychiatrist. It was for her own use when her back hurt.

I recalled that the first time I met Celine, in medical school, was during one of her exacerbations of back pain. We were in anatomy class, working on our cadavers in groups of five. Our professor, Dr.

William Warring, one of the biggest chauvinists on the faculty during that era, marched up and down the aisles between the corpses, offering comments such as, "If any of the ladies feel faint, for God's sake say so." When the class was over, my group was the last to finish putting our equipment away. Jessica, whom I had met in a physiology lecture a few days before, waited for me. As we walked across the sprawling anatomy lab, we noticed a red-headed woman standing alone and very still, but at an odd angle, next to one of the cadavers near the door. "Are you OK?" Jessica asked her.

She gave a barely perceptible nod and grimaced.

Jessica and I introduced ourselves, and she said, through gritted teeth, that she was Celine Byrd. Moving only her extraocular muscles, she watched Dr. Warring as he traversed the lab and walked out the door. She looked so uncomfortable that I asked, "You sure you don't need any help?"

"I coughed and threw my back out," she answered, as immobile as a statue. Then she clamped her jaw and staggered toward the door, her back twisted and her eyes watering. "Thanks," she breathed. "I didn't want—," she winced with each step, "that sexist—to think— I needed—any—help." Despite the inauspicious beginning, she excelled at anatomy.

Celine sat down on the sofa, after switching on the ceiling light, and I took one of the chairs in front of her desk.

"Something terrible is happening," she said, reaching up to push the door closed.

"I'm sorry."

"You don't know what it is yet," she said, a little perplexed. She leaned forward anxiously. "Do you?"

"Oh. No," I said.

"It's been going on for about two weeks, but I haven't told anyone because I wasn't sure what to do."

It's probably been going on longer than that, I thought.

"I haven't even told Frank," she said.

I wondered how she found out.

"Well, because the first time I had sciatica, I did take a lot of Vicodin. I was in so much pain."

Now I was lost. "What?"

"Look at this," she said, and she walked around to the front of her desk and unlocked the top left-hand drawer. I stood up and leaned over the desktop to look. In the drawer, lined up in neat rows, were five bottles of morphine and two of Dilaudid.

It took a minute to sink in that I was looking at the Medical Center's missing narcotics. I gawked at the opened drawer, and she closed it. "How did that get there?"

"In the drawer? I put it there. The question is, how did it get in my brief case and my coat pockets? Every few days I find another bottle or two." She circled her desk and looked around her office, as if expecting a vial to pop out of the wall. "Yesterday I took a glove out of my coat pocket, and pulled out some Dilaudid with it. I had to hide it in my palm, and I'm not sure whether anyone saw it."

"Well, you have to report it!" I was flabbergasted. "You have to tell someone! You have the missing narcotics!"

"Please, Nora, don't shout," she said. I stood up, and she sat back down on the sofa. "Who should I tell?"

"I don't know, Martin Baxter!"

"What if he doesn't believe I found them? What if he thinks I stole them?"

"Well, if you stole them, why would you report it?"

"Nora, it's easy for you to say. Who would ever suspect you of abusing opiates?"

"I don't understand."

"I've taken a lot of narcotics in the past few years for my back."

"So what?"

"Maybe not everyone would think, 'So what?'"

I couldn't believe it. "Are you addicted?" I asked.

"No, but I've been out sick a lot. Don't you think people would think I stole them?"

"No."

"The truth is," she murmured, "Frank might."

"Frank thinks you're addicted?"

"I don't think so, but I know that he's worried about it before."

I was becoming exasperated. "Celine, do you have a drug problem or not?" I demanded.

"No, of course not," she said. "I have a saint-for-a-husband problem."

Well, if that didn't beat all.

"You know what he's like," she continued. "He's such a straight arrow, he wouldn't even take a Tylenol for a headache, wouldn't even know he *had* a headache because he's too busy devoting himself to his patients, or the twins, or me." She pressed her temples as if she had a whopping headache herself, and I certainly was getting one.

"What you're saying isn't rational. You have to tell someone you have the narcotics. They have to be returned! What if somebody finds them before you say anything, Celine?"

She didn't answer me. I asked her if she knew of any nurse who had a grudge against her.

"No, why do you think it's a nurse?"

"Actually, I don't. But whoever it is has access to the narcotics keys. How about a resident, or one of the psychiatry fellows? Have you written any negative reference letters?" She hadn't. "Well, the important thing is to come forward. Then you'll be off the hook." I started pacing around her office. "Whoever is doing this to you will stop. It must be some psycho. You know plenty of those."

"Thanks," she said grimly.

"Maybe it's some disgruntled patient trying to get you in trouble, who knows?"

"Nora, please let me deal with this my own way. I'm not ready to tell anyone besides you."

I was still treading back and forth. "Do you hang your coat up here or in the doctors' lounge?" I asked.

"Doctors' lounge." She left her briefcase there sometimes, too, including in the past two weeks. "I've got a plan," she announced. I regarded her with disbelief. "I've written a letter."

"Oh, my God," I said, standing still.

"I've left it in my coat pocket, so my harasser will find it." She leaned against the wall, apparently finished with her explanation.

"And? So? What do you mean 'find it?' What does it say?"

She shrugged. "It says I've paid a private security company to install a camera in the cloak room, that's not really true, so that the person reading the letter is now on videotape. But if that person agrees to discreetly, say, in the middle of the night, remove the narcotics from my desk drawer, and put them back where they belong, *and never bother me again*—underlined—I won't reveal their identity."

"Oh God," I moaned, and sat back down. She was coming unhinged. "I can't say I think that's a good idea. Why do you assume they'll take out the note. Does it say, 'To My Harrasser'?"

Celine didn't answer.

"This might be really dangerous, Celine. Anyway, how would they get into your office, and the desk drawer?"

"I'm leaving my office door unlocked at night. I don't keep anything very valuable in here. If anyone wants an issue of the *American Journal of Psychiatry*, they can have it. And I've put a copy of the key to the drawer in the envelope."

"You mean you've done this already?"

"Yes, I told you. This morning, when I hung up my coat."

Neither of us spoke for the next few minutes. I recommended walking up and down the length of her office. "Of course, I can't say anything because it will cast suspicion on you," I finally ruminated out loud.

"I would appreciate it if you didn't."

"The police would be much more likely to solve this than you." I started to wring my hands. "Please, please take it to Martin. He's easy to talk to."

She wouldn't budge. "Why did you tell me this?" I asked.

"I had to tell someone," she said, "and you know Frank so well, I hoped you'd understand my predicament."

"I think you're making a big mistake, Celine," I said.

"I'm sorry you think so," was her reply.

"Maybe there's still time to take the letter back from your coat pocket."

"Don't you dare touch my coat pocket, Nora!" she said. "That's not why I told you this." Despite her apparent confidence in her wacky plan, it was obvious she was distressed. It was also obvious that I would be unable to dissuade her.

Celine rose from the sofa and said, "I've got to get back to the unit." I looked at my watch and saw that I was already ten minutes late for noon conference, all the way over on the second floor of the South Building. Roman was presenting a case of inflammatory bowel disease from our service, and I should have been there when he started. I told Celine we'd have to finish talking later and heard her say she was finished as I flew out the door and down the corridor to the elevator. It didn't come right away, so I took the stairs, running down eleven flights to the basement and through the tunnels. Maybe it was better that I didn't have time to reflect on what I had learned. Ironic, I thought, how much worse it was than what I had been afraid of.

For mysterious reasons, noon conference, which was catered and therefore uniquely popular, was held in a room that was too small to accommodate the crowd. When I arrived, late, every chair was taken and people lined the walls. My team was loyally ensconced in the first row, and Paul had saved me a seat that I claimed with some embarrassment, though not enough to bypass the food table. Roman sat in a folding chair at the front of the room, next to Ken Smiley, the chief resident who was running the conference. Ken stood at the blackboard, writing down pertinent information as Roman spoke. Sitting up front by the door were Xavier Bennett, the residency program director, Irwin Liu, my boss at PCIMC, Wally Todd, several other senior faculty members, and the other three chief residents. The rest of the attendings and housestaff were commingled throughout the room. As I took a paper plate and helped myself to a sandwich, Roman finished reciting the physical exam and started the laboratory results, beginning with the x-rays. Ken switched on the lights in the two view boxes on the wall, next to the blackboard, picked up an X-ray folder from the floor, and put up two films. Someone sitting near the wall light switch turned it off. Then, in another absurd Lafayette conference ritual, everyone stampeded forward to take a look, ensuring that only the handful that got there first would be able to see anything.

"Someone please tell us what kind of study this is," Ken said, standing next to the view boxes and pointing at one of the films. The request by itself was unobjectionable, but Ken's manner was a combination of pedantry and ambition that could set your teeth on edge. One of the residents up front must have answered, because Ken's next comment was, "Right, a double contrast barium enema." I added a spoonful of potato salad to my plate. "You can see the mucosal thickening, and the ulceration of the wall of the colon." I looked up, but it was impossible to see anything. Ken pointed to the other view box and said, "This is from, let's see, this should be from two years ago," he scanned the corners of the film, "Yeah, here it is, July 1989, OK. What you can see here is a number of small, early erosions, here, here, here, all these little areas where the barium collects." Everyone wanted to see these, so there was a lot of craning, twisting and murmuring. Then Ken took the films down and the audience returned to its seats. Roman concluded with the rest of the laboratory results, and Ken began his discussion of the case, with, of course, a slide presentation.

I advanced to the front row and sat down, balancing my plate on my lap, as Ken showed us a slide listing the causes of bloody diarrhea. We lunched as he showed us pictures from sigmoidoscopies, slides of intestinal biopsies, and photographs of resected colons, the glistening, bumpy organs displayed against a backdrop of Pathology Department blue.

"Beautiful photographs," Xavier murmured.

Then Ken reviewed the available therapies, and ended with a discussion of our patient's medical regimen and likely prognosis. It turned out she had a poor track record for taking her medications and keeping follow-up appointments. When Ken finished, Elliot Chertoff, a senior faculty member from the division of gastroenterology asked what was the patient's nationality.

"American," Roman answered.

"I meant her ethnicity," Elliot persisted. He had just published his third book on culture and medicine and was considered an authority on the subject of cultural competence, still relatively new in 1991. It was based on the idea that a discrepancy always existed between a patient's experience of illness and the doctor's response to it, since each was influenced by the culture and beliefs of the patient and doctor, respectively. By asking the right questions, discarding stereotypes, and, above all, approaching each patient with sensitivity and respect, a doctor can become "competent" in caring for patients from different cultures. The problem with Elliott was that he was rather attached to stereotypes, especially when they had to do with gender, and his questions always seemed to be formulated with a book chapter in mind.

"Estonian," Roman answered. Paul and I looked at each other quizzically. If Roman knew this, we certainly didn't.

"And were you able to explore her cultural biases regarding intestinal disease?" Elliot peered at Roman over the top of his reading glasses. He was leaning back in his seat, his left arm dangling behind him over the top of the chair. His long, curly gray hair was pulled back in a ponytail.

Roman didn't answer.

"Of course it would be important to do that, Dr. Chertoff," Ken chirped.

"Frankly," Elliot continued, now taking his glasses off and spinning them around, "I'm not surprised at the number of relapses this unfortunate patient has already had, despite therapy. Nor am I optimistic about her prognosis."

"Do Estonians with inflammatory bowel disease usually have a bad prognosis?" Roman asked.

"Physicians," Elliot scoffed, springing forward, "who treat patients simply as organ systems, without respect to the cultural context unique to each individual, and expressed within that individual's cultural community, guarantee a bad prognosis."

Roman thought for a moment. "Oh. I get it," he nodded. "But that's not how we treated her."

"We all have plenty to learn from Dr. Chertoff's extensive experience in the area of cultural competence," Ken hastened to add.

"Apparently," Elliott observed, "no one has taken the time to probe her attitude toward, for example, taking prescribed medications."

"She'd like to take—" Roman began, but Elliott cut him off.

"Or what her belief system is regarding healers. Why doesn't she keep her appointments with her physicians?"

"She lost her ins—"

"What are the things in her life from which she derives meaning? What are her spiritual resources? How does she perceive her illness in the context of her cultural beliefs?"

"She wants to get back to work," Roman said. "That's the main thing."

"She works?" Elliott was surprised. "Did you tell us that in your history?"

"Yes, I'm sure I did. She's a cocktail waitress."

"A cocktail waitress? What's her husband doing?"

"She doesn't have a husband," Roman replied.

"Did you say that in the social history?" Elliott asked, irritated.

"Yes."

"Well, I must have missed it. I thought you said she has four children."

"I did," Roman said, "but she was never married."

"That's possible, you know, Elliott," Xavier quipped. There was polite, subdued laughter. Elliott was a tenured professor and member of several influential committees at the medical school and hospital, and people were intimidated by him.

"Well," Elliott said, shifting again in his chair. "If she's an unmarried cocktail waitress, mother of four that may explain her difficulty complying with medical regimens." He was right, I thought, but not in the way he intended. "I wasn't aware," he added, "that that kind of thing is condoned in the Estonian community."

Jessica's hand shot up in the air, and I groaned silently—No, Jessica, just let us get out of here. Fortunately Xavier, without turning around, said, "Well, thank you, Ken, for a very interesting presentation," ending the conference.

Our team waited for Roman as everyone began filing out of the conference room. "Nice job," Paul told him, slapping him on the back.

"Very nice, Roman," I agreed. "I'm sorry I missed the beginning. I got stuck on the psychiatry floor."

"That's OK, Dr. S.," Roman said, adding, "I didn't really understand what Dr. Chertoff was saying at the end."

"Don't worry about it," I told him.

"Well, I understood it," Michelle said. "He was saying she's an irresponsible patient because she has four children and no husband." When I didn't comment she said, "Don't you think that's what he meant, Dr. Sternberg?"

"One might interpret it that way," I said, trying to sound nonjudgmental.

Paul said they all had a lot of work to do, and he would page me at the end of the day to "run the list," meaning go over our patients before we left the hospital. As they headed in the direction of Schilling Three, I located Jessica, who had been waiting for me outside the conference room.

"What did you think of that?" she asked me.

"Roman did a great job," I said. "And I kept thinking it was a good thing he was presenting the case and not Michelle. Elliott might have gotten nasty."

"Now he has a new case report for his next book: the sick Estonian slut . But I have something more important to tell you," she whispered as we navigated the traffic in the corridor. "You'll never guess who's in the hospital!"

After my conversation with Celine, I didn't know how much more intrigue I could take.

"It's not a secret, is it?"

"No. Secret? What do you mean?"

"Never mind," I said.

"Your Mrs. Townsend is on Schilling Five!"

"Mrs. Townsend of the late Dr. Townsend?"

"The same."

"How do you know?"

"Because we were called to do a consult!" She could barely contain her excitement. An elderly widow named Ida Townsend, whose late husband had formerly been on staff at Lafayette, was admitted with a change in mental status. She was found to be hyperthyroid, prompting the request for an endocrinology consultation.

"When are you going to see her?" I asked. I had to admit I felt a little keyed up myself.

Jessica answered that the endocrine fellow was seeing her already, and she would join him shortly. A medical consultation begins with a history and physical examination, so Jessica had, in essence, been invited to a private interview with the widow of Harris Townsend.

"It's unbelievable luck," she said.

"Well, not for Mrs. Townsend."

"That's true."

"What are you going to ask her?"

"I guess it depends how wifty she is," Jessica said thoughtfully. "They said she's back at her baseline mental status, but who knows what that is." By "they" she meant the Schilling Five housestaff who had requested the consultation.

"Find out if Townsend had a nickname, you know, if he was short, or incredibly handsome. And find out if he knew my aunt."

"I'll certainly try."

Although I was highly pleased with this development, I was also a little leery that we might be doing something more or less unethical. We were exploiting the circumstances of her illness—that was incontrovertible. What were the NATCH standards in a case like this? It wasn't exactly a violation of patient confidentiality in the usual sense, but we were using the privileged interview to dig around in territory that had no bearing on her well being. As I watched Jessica plow through the hallway toward the stairs I inferred that she wasn't torturing herself with the moral issue.

It was a busy day for the Schilling Three team. After Roman's talk we met in the Pathology Department in the sub-basement of the South Building to view the peripheral blood smear from a patient on our service with lead toxicity. As we jammed into the hematologist's office, I noticed Roberta Garrett walking briskly ahead of us down the cinder-block-lined hallway. The sight of her made me think of Frank, which inevitably led to thoughts of Celine, which made me shut them both out of my mind so I could do my work. I wanted to get back to the floor and finish my charts before the monthly department of medicine meeting at 5:30, so that I could go home after the meeting, pour myself a Scotch from Brad's supply, and knock myself out.

CHAPTER NINE

The department of medicine meeting is like a play re-enacted every month with the same script. We even sit in the same seats in the department conference room on Three South. I duly took my seat by the window overlooking the South Building garage as we all filed in for the February performance. Wally opened the first act, "Productivity," as he always does, by standing before the assembled physicians and exhorting us to see more patients. No matter how many we saw, we fell short of the productivity standard for the department, determined by the president and senior vice-presidents of the hospital. Of these top administrators, one was a doctor and he last practiced medicine in the 1970's. Wally distributed hand-outs that showed monthly department productivity figures, broken down by subspecialty, depicted in bar graphs, compared to past months, computed as percentages above (theoretically) and below (actually) the target levels, and indicating the excess number of patients that needed to be seen in the remaining months of the year to make up for the shortfall to date. Since it was only February, the number was still relatively low.

"I'm sure we can all think of ways to increase our efficiency and speed up patient visits," Wally said. "The current standard, as I believe everyone knows, is four patients an hour. That's fifteen minutes per patient. There's no reason we can't meet that number comfortably."

Members of the audience coughed and shifted in their seats. As usual, it was the PCIMC doctors who spoke up. We felt the most vulnerable because the clinic, with its relatively small share of commercially-insured patients, was always a loss for the hospital. For this reason, I suppose, and unlike the members of the other divisions, we tended to sit together, presenting a unified front.

"Wally, many of the patients in my panel are geriatric," Lance Nichols, one of my PCIMC colleagues said. "It takes them eleven minutes to get in the room and take their coats off. That leaves just four minutes for the visit."

"So in that case," Wally countered, "your challenge, as a division within the department, because I'm giving you wide latitude with this—" Lance, sitting with his arms folded across his chest, regarded Wally skeptically, "—is to figure out how to move the patients in and out faster. Why isn't your medical assistant getting each patient ready, undressed, whatever, in your second room while you're finishing the patient in the first room? That would save you forty-four minutes an hour."

"OK, Wally," Lance said. I could tell by the sound of his voice that he was taking the gloves off. "I don't always have two rooms. It depends on how many attendings and residents are assigned to clinic on a particular day. Often I have one room. And even when I do have two, my medical assistant is likely to be tied up translating for another doctor, or doing referrals, or looking for the chart. So half the time I end up putting the patient in the room myself." The rest of us nodded in agreement.

It was now time for my boss, Irwin Liu, to provide a reality check. "Keep in mind, Wally, that our patients have a high number of co-morbidities. So our average diabetic, hypertensive, depressed patient with heart disease who smokes is going to need a lot of things done at each follow-up visit: weight, blood pressure, fingerstick glucose, inspection of the feet, some discussion about diet, exercise, and tobacco cessation, review of medications, renewal of prescriptions, etc. And that's assuming they're not sick."

"There's no time for anyone to be sick," Lance interjected.

If they get sick their HMO will spit them out like poison, I thought. And I immediately gritted my teeth, because I knew what was coming next.

"Again, as we've discussed at previous meetings," Wally said in a tone that indicated we were trying his patience mightily, "there's no reason to do everything at one visit. Do a little at a time and schedule return appointments for the rest. That is, assuming they're not in a capitated plan."

Now I had my dilemma. Should I speak up and tick Wally off and probably annoy everyone else, who would just like the discussion to end, or should I let it go? Let it go, I thought.

"But it's an expense and it's often difficult for many patients to get here," I heard myself saying.

"It's certainly not an expense for the ones on Medicaid," Wally retorted.

"Even for the ones on Medicaid," I persisted. "There's transportation, there may be childcare needs. And many of the people who work don't get paid for time off."

"Thank you, Nora, for reminding us of that," Wally said stiffly. Then readdressing the whole audience, he continued, "I'll be the first to acknowledge that this is a challenge, for all of us." He must have been using the royal "us," since Wally only saw patients one half-day a week, in the faculty practice offices that occupied their own building across the street from the South Building. According to Jessica, who also worked in the faculty practice, Wally always got more help from the support staff than anyone else. "I believe that we all share the same goal: to see the Medical Center continue to flourish. Increasingly, and I say this with regret, the success of the institution depends on our ability to drive up the numbers. That's the reality in 1991. We're simply not seeing enough patients. And I would answer the PCIMC folks—" Here I winced. I hated it when he used the word "folks," pretending to be folksy as he twisted the knife in our backs. He had ruined that word for me. "—we're not serving the community very well if we limit access to health care." As if we were the ones limiting access. The charge was so absurd we let it go, almost.

Andy Redman, another PCIMC colleague, said, "Since you've

mentioned access, Wally, could you explain the policy on specialty clinic referrals for uninsured patients?" This was one of those burning PCIMC issues that no one else in the institution gave a hoot about. We, the PCIMC doctors, suspected that the Medical Center was constructing invisible barriers to keep our low-income uninsured patients out of its specialty and subspecialty clinics. One method, for instance, was to have receptionists "remind" patients on the phone that they would be expected to pay an up-front fee of two-hundred dollars for the first visit, a practice that our patients reported to us and that we suspected might violate federal regulations. Andy posed the question in such a calm, gentlemanly way that you'd never suspect the resentment the topic engendered at our division meetings.

"The Medical Center treats uninsured patients exactly the same as insured patients, Andy," Wally proclaimed with a straight face. I saw Irwin mouth the word "data," his mantra, in an aside. He was right that we needed the data to make our case, and that the data would bear us out, no less than the truth would set us free. But the unassailable reality was that our clinic didn't bring in any cash for the institution, and money ruled.

Wally shuffled some papers in front of him and we all braced ourselves for what we knew was coming next.

"The hospital is proceeding," he continued, "with plans to implement pay incentivization for full-time staff." The room broke out in a chorus of grumbling and gnashing of teeth that Wally pretended not to hear. "I know rumors have been circulating about this issue, and I would like, once more, to try to dispel them. In essence, each of you will be paid a baseline salary that will be supplemented, or not, according to how many patients you see annually."

"Regardless of diagnosis, of complexity?" Irwin asked.

"For now, yes," Wally said. "Ultimately that will change."

In these and other Medical Center meetings, discussions about our practice were so consistently focused on productivity, as defined by numbers, that to suggest we should be measuring quality of care almost seemed in bad taste. Nonetheless, a stalwart from our ranks, Alice Cummings from the division of infectious diseases, couldn't restrain herself from raising her hand. "Yes, Alice," Wally sighed.

"In our zeal to boost the numbers," Alice said, "how will we find sufficient time to teach the residents and fellows we are responsible for training in our clinics?" I imagine if someone my age had put the question to Wally he would have been offended. But Alice, who was one of the very few woman attendings at Lafayette older than fifty, and who was even more of a fixture at the Medical Center than Wally, could do it with impunity. And of course, this was her role in the script.

Wally reassured us that the residents would continue to have thirty minutes per patient in PCIMC, omitting any discussion of the subspecialty clinics, and that the supervising attendings would be given ample time to precept. No one was reassured.

"And then you'll pay me less because I'm slowing down the assembly line," Alice complained.

"What about research time?" This question was posed by Arnold Sweet, one of the rheumatologists, who had come to Lafayette from

Chicago two years earlier. He had a big NIH grant, and recruiting him was considered a coup for the Medical Center.

"Of course you will still have your research time," Wally replied. "The administration is totally committed to maintaining our position as a premier research institution. Totally committed."

"I would like to see that same level of commitment to maintaining excellence in teaching," Alice quipped. Wally ignored her.

End Act I. Begin Act II, "Liability," which contains some improvisation. Wally introduced a member of the NATCH survey preparation committee from human resources, who handed out schedules of training sessions we were required to attend before the survey. The topics for the day included patient confidentiality and hazardous waste disposal. She was followed by Martin Baxter with the QUELL update. Martin looked strangely calm, leading me to wonder if he had premedicated himself for the meeting. Once he started his report, it was clear that we all should have been premedicated.

"Yesterday two vials of morphine were discovered missing from the narcotics box on Trilling Two," he announced. A groan went up from the crowd. Trilling Two was a surgical floor. The thief was branching out.

Milton Black, an elder member of the department, barked at Martin from the front row, "Who the hell's running this investigation?"

Without a flicker of a tic, Martin replied that a team reporting directly to the risk management office was working on it nonstop.

"Risk Management? What about the police?" Milton asked.

The faintest shadow passed over Martin's face. "Mr. Irnings is meeting daily with Risk Management, and the consensus is that the police shouldn't be called in at this point." Mr. Irnings was the president and C.E.O. of Lafayette Medical Center. I had never met him although I had seen him from a distance once or twice at major hospital functions. I recognized him from the head shot that appeared with his column, "My Finger on the Pulse" in the quarterly *Lafayette Medical Center Bulletin*. He didn't set foot on the wards or in the clinic, but rather traveled in a parallel universe of top brass that existed somewhere unseen by rank–and-file doctors.

Wally, who had also taken a seat in the first row, returned to the front of the room and stood at the podium next to Martin. "The administration is particularly concerned about the proximity to the NATCH survey," he elaborated. "Any publicity at this time would be highly undesirable." Coughs, murmurs, and the sounds of bodies squirming in their seats could be heard.

"Do you think this isn't going to leak out?" Milton demanded. "It would be much better if the hospital reported the thefts. Imagine how it will look when it comes out that we knew about it and kept it from the police."

"Milton, you're certainly free to take that up with Bill Shell," Martin said, referring to Dr. Shell, the Chief of Services, more or less the head doctor at the Medical Center. "Or with Bob Schift." His title was Vice President for Clinical Operations, whatever that meant.

"I'll take it up with Don Irnings," Milton said, exasperated.

"Or Don Irnings."

Martin sat down, smiling serenely, and I had the bizarre thought that perhaps he was the narcotics thief and the QUELL chairmanship was a front. Or maybe someone else was the thief and he was the fence. As I was considering these unlikely possibilities, Wally concluded the meeting.

"On a lighter note," he said, flashing one of his trademark split-second, humorless smiles, "I want to remind everyone that there's still time to buy tickets to Griffin Garrett's dinner. Also, don't forget the reception Thursday afternoon in the Treemont conference room. It's being given by the neurosurgery department, and everyone should have received an invitation." There was a low buzz of conversation. "These are important events for the Medical Center," Wally continued, "and we want the department of medicine to be well-represented."

With that, the meeting came to an end, and we all filed out into the corridor, thoroughly depressed.

As everyone milled around, shaking his or her head, I waited for Jessica. I was anxious to hear about the Townsend consultation. She finally emerged from the conference room, talking to Milton Black, and broke free when she saw me.

"Why does it always have to be such a bummer?" she asked softly.

"Because it's always the same meeting," I said, steering us around the traffic in the hallway.

"That's what Ray says."

"Where is Ray? I didn't see him."

"Frieda's got a cold. Couldn't go to daycare, so we split the day. I stayed home this morning and Ray took the afternoon."

"I hope she's all right," I said.

Jessica nodded. "She'll be fine. But next Drew will get it, and we'll have to do the same thing all over again."

"Did you get a chance to see Mrs. Townsend?"

"I did, and I'm sorry I got your hopes up," she said. "It was a disappointment."

"Was it the right Mrs. Townsend?"

"Oh yeah. Her late husband was the anesthesiologist, all right, but she didn't want to talk about him."

"So did you find out anything?"

"Well," Jessica said, "they didn't have any children. They lived in an apartment on the Upper East Side, and for many years they owned a vacation house on Cape Cod, but about a year ago they sold it. Her chief interest is gambling—"

"Gambling?" I stopped her. "You mean like Atlantic City?"

"That's exactly what I mean. She takes the bus there whenever she can. The doctor had disapproved, and I got the distinct impression that she had intended to visit the casinos more frequently after his death, but then her health started to deteriorate. And to make it a total waste," she concluded, "she wasn't even hyperthyroid."

"Were you able to find out anything about my aunt?" I asked.

"It's funny, that's the only thing that really got her attention. I called her 'Miss Sternberg' once, as if I had forgotten her name, and she almost fell out of the bed. She said '*What* did you call me?' but I couldn't get anything else out of her."

"Was she with it?"

"Completely."

Jessica's beeper went off, and she crossed the corridor to pick up the house phone on the wall. As I waited for her, I caught a glimpse of Frank down the hallway, stepping into one of the South Building elevators. I hadn't seen him since our conversation in the doctors' lounge. When he spotted me he waved and flashed a wide, significant smile. Somehow I knew what this meant. He was signaling that he had ended his relationship with Roberta Garrett. I smiled back, but couldn't help thinking this jovial camaraderie would be put to the test once Celine got busted.

Jessica hung up the phone and said, "The kids are screaming and Ray's losing it. I have to go home." I was ready to leave, too. We walked down the stairs to the second floor and took the escalator to the atrium. Then Jessica turned north toward her office, and I stopped in the doctors' lounge to get my coat from the cloakroom, momentarily considering searching through all the many coats to see if Celine's was there. Instead, I gripped sanity tightly and walked out.

As soon as I reached home I opened the kitchen cabinet where we kept the alcohol and poured out a small glass of Scotch, with ice. I sat on the living room sofa and drank it down. Townsend and Aunt Selma were connected, that was certain, but in what way, or ways? There was something else that had been nagging at me for a couple of days, something I had seen that I couldn't remember. It came to me now. I had watched a visitor enter Margaret Eichling's room a little after eight o'clock in the morning, a time when there are very few visitors. I couldn't remember seeing the person leave the room, but they must have, because no one was there when we all crowded in for the code.

It was all extremely confusing. I closed my eyes, thinking I probably shouldn't go to sleep, and drifted off. When I awoke with the bright ceiling lamp glaring down at me, it was almost eleven o'clock. I got up and washed my face, and was about to make something to eat, when I remembered that there were two notes I hadn't finished on Schilling Three. I meant to go back to the floor after the department of medicine meeting and had forgotten. Well, the hospital would still be standing in the morning, I reasoned, if my notes for the day were unwritten. On the other hand, one of the two I missed was a patient with AIDS, and I had not gone over him on rounds as carefully as I should have, though he was doing well. But just when you relax is when all hell breaks loose. I went back and forth in my head like that, and finally decided to just get it over with and go back to the hospital.

CHAPTER TEN

The lobby was deserted, of course, but as I waited for the elevator to Schilling Three I was surprised to see Martin Baxter walking hurriedly toward the South Building stairs. I called to him, and he turned around, at least as surprised to see me. He said he was covering the invasive cardiology service and had been called in for an emergency cardiac catheterization. Without asking what I was doing at the hospital at eleven o'clock at night, he waved and vanished into the stairwell. I could understand that he was in a rush, but the cath lab was in the opposite direction.

Seconds later, who should come jogging across the atrium but Frank, heading toward the corridor that led to the Tower Building. I ran to the atrium to catch up with him and said, "Frank, what are you doing here?"

He was astonished to see me. "H-hi, Nora. I'm on-call and they paged me to the NICU," by which he meant the neonatal ICU. "Gotta run," and he sped off down the corridor.

Pondering these unexpected encounters, I arrived on Schilling Three where Mrs. Pierre, the night clerk, was the only person in evidence. As she had done since my medical school days, she presided over the console at the nursing station that was connected to the intercom in each patient room. "Hello, Nora, what are you doing here at this hour?" she asked in her gentle Haitian accent.

I told her I had to see two patients, and it was good to know she was still holding Schilling Three together. As we spoke, I scanned the chart rack for the two charts I needed, and noticed something odd. I recognized the name of a patient followed in PCIMC, but the name on the chart was Fabricant. Since the patient was on Medicaid, she should have been admitted to one of the housestaff teaching services, such as mine. Leon Fabricant, however, didn't attend on the teaching service. I removed the chart from the rack and opened it. The patient's name was Mildred Downey, and her date-of-birth was July 9, 1905. She had been admitted after being found on the floor (FOF in intern-abbreviated parlance), and, sure enough, there was an attending admission note signed by Fabricant.

I heard giggling and looked up to see none other than Leon himself ambling toward the nursing station accompanied by a female resident, each of them with a paper cup of coffee. The only place you could get coffee in the hospital at that hour was the machine in the doctors' lounge, and the thought of Leon fraternizing with the female housestaff was unsettling. He produced his phony grin as he leaned against the counter. I didn't know what to do with the chart lying open before me. For once there wasn't a single chart strewn around the counter that I could slide it under. Fabricant walked inside the nursing station and surveyed the chart rack.

"Hello, Dr. Fabricant," Mrs. Pierre said pleasantly.

"Hello," he answered, turning toward the counter and eyeing the chart in front of me. "That's not Downey's chart, is it?" he drawled.

"Yes, it is."

"Are you finished with it?" He had abruptly stopped smiling, and I thought, here we go again.

"What are you doing making rounds at this hour, Leon?" I asked.

"Oh, I was out of town for the day, so I'm just coming in now," he said nonchalantly, taking the chart from me. The resident, also flipping through a chart on the counter, shifted her weight from one foot to the other self-consciously. I wondered why Leon didn't have someone in his covering group round for him if he was away.

The phone lines on Mrs. Pierre's console started ringing. Through static so thick you would think the call was coming from the other side of the earth, a voice whimpered, "I need more pain medication."

Mrs. Pierre leaned over the microphone and said, "I'll tell your nurse right away." She ran her finger down a piece of paper she kept by the phone, then pushed a button on the console and spoke into the microphone, "Dolores, location, please."

The console rang again and another patient said she needed a bedpan. Dolores responded that she was in room twenty-five. Mrs. Pierre hit the intercom and repeated the request for pain medication.

Dolores said she was moving twenty-five-A to a stretcher to go down to x-ray and would get the medication next. Mrs. Pierre deftly pushed another button and said, "She'll be with you as soon as she can, Mr. Schuller." No doubt Mr. Schuller was unaware that the hospital had cut back on nursing staff, leaving Dolores and the other nurse to cover the entire floor for the shift, each with seventeen patients. He'd get the gist of it after awhile.

Fabricant was standing next to my chair, reading the chart. "I know Mrs. Downey from clinic," I said. "I assumed she was on my service."

"No, she's on my service," he said without looking at me.

The bell on the console pealed again, and the need for a bedpan was reiterated with greater urgency.

"That's wonderful, Leon," I said. "I didn't know you've started taking Medicaid patients." I admit it was snide. Fabricant seeing a patient on Medicaid was as likely as the dissolution of the HMOs, which would surely herald the coming of the Messiah.

"I didn't know she had Medicaid," he said, concentrating on the chart as he flipped through it. This was so preposterous I nearly gasped.

"Could I please have another Percocet?" A new, high-frequency voice wobbled over the console.

"Peggy, location," Mrs. Pierre spoke into the microphone.

"Did she ever work at the hospital?" I asked him.

He still didn't look up. "Yes, I believe she did."

"Fourteen," Peggy called, "I'm inserting a Foley catheter." After a few seconds she said, "Mrs. Pierre, please call Mrs. Stevens and tell her we need a float."

Mrs. Pierre sighed and said, "I already did."

"And?"

Mr. Schuller was back. "Is the nurse coming soon?"

"She's helping another patient. She'll be there as soon as she can," Mrs. Pierre improvised. She pushed the room fourteen intercom button again. "She said she doesn't have anybody. There are already nurses floating in the CCU and on Schilling Five. She's calling people on the day shift to see if anyone can come in early."

"I don't think the hospital has enough nurses," a thin voice floated faintly over the intercom. With that, a thunderous crash followed by a prolonged metallic clattering, and a voice screaming, "Help me!" echoed down the hall. We all jumped up and ran in the direction of the noise, which had issued from room sixteen. Peggy rushed in, pulling Betadine-stained gloves off her hands. We found a patient sprawled on the floor, half inside and half out of the bathroom, her hospital gown billowing around her, a pool of fluid expanding outward under the gown, and a walker and IV pole on their sides, blocking the door.

"I couldn't wait," she screamed. "I told you I had to go!" Peggy, Mrs. Pierre, and I picked our way through the equipment cluttering the floor, trying to avoid the puddle. When we attempted to lift her the screaming intensified.

Leon stepped into the rubble, saying, "Here, let me pick her up." He grasped the patient under the axillae and hoisted her vertically.

Peggy grabbed her feet, and they deposited her on the bed.

"Thanks, Dr. Fabricant," Peggy panted. Leon nodded, breathing heavily, and then fled the room. Peggy slipped out and returned carrying a bedpan.

"I don't need it anymore," the patient yelled.

Peggy rolled her on her side and pushed the bedpan under her, saying briskly, "You never know, there might be more."

"Ow! I think you broke my hip!"

We examined her hips and legs and I said, "I don't think anything's broken." The patient, who had an absolute minimum of flesh on her bones, and was probably in her mid-to-late nineties, seemed a good candidate for a fracture. Peggy patted her on the arm, eliciting a yelp of pain, and said she would get a fresh gown and make her comfortable. With that we left the room. I said to Peggy, "You better get the intern to come look at her, and maybe get some x-rays."

She nodded. "First I have to finish Mrs. Gilroy's Foley," and she returned to room fourteen. Mrs. Pierre was back in her chair, calling housekeeping.

A stretcher carrying a patient rounded the corner of the north corridor, pushed by a transporter in green scrubs, and followed by Dolores. She was heading for the medication room. Another patient line started ringing, and a new voice, a soprano, trilled over the console, "I can't br . . ."

She was drowned out by a lengthy, phlegmatic spasm of coughing from the same room.

The first patient tried again, "I can't brea . . ."

"Aaach! Oogh. Pftzch!" The coughing stopped, and a barrage of giant, wet spitting sounds could be heard.

"What's she trying to say?" Dolores called to Mrs. Pierre from the threshold of the medication room.

"I can't make it out."

"Who is it?"

"Um . . ." Mrs. Pierre consulted the white board on the opposite wall, on which a grid containing all the room numbers, patients' names, and their doctors' and nurses' names was drawn. This display of confidential information was usually at least a day old. "I think it's Sullivan."

"Oh. Tell her I'll be right there." Dolores pulled the ring of keys from her hip and opened the medication room door, which swung shut behind her.

"She'll be right with you, Mrs. Sullivan," Mrs. Pierre spoke into the console.

The cough started up again, crackling over the intercom like a round of artillery fire.

Mrs. Pierre leaned into the console and asked, "Who's coughing?"

"I can't bre . . ."

Mrs. Pierre scanned the white board again.

"Is it you, Mrs. Portense?"

Dolores popped out of the medication room and said to Mrs. Pierre, "I think I'm mixing up Sullivan with someone else. Can you see if she's OK?"

Mrs. Pierre pushed a button and said, "Are you all right, Mrs. Sullivan?"

No answer. "She's not answering." Meanwhile the coughing had degenerated into a series of loud wheezes followed by more hacking and gagging.

Dolores sighed and headed in Mrs. Sullivan's direction. I followed, and entered the room next door where my patient, Ms. Milagros Sepulveda, was fortunately still awake, perhaps not so surprising considering all the noise. She sat up obligingly and let me listen to her lungs and heart, and thanked me for coming to see her. When I left her room I walked back in the direction of the nursing station, and noticed that Mrs. Pierre was not at her post. I stepped into the room of the last patient on my list, Mr. Cornell Dobbs, a twenty-four year-old AIDS patient. He appeared to be asleep, so I watched him for a minute, counting his respirations. He whispered, "I'm awake."

"How do you feel, Cornell?" I whispered back, stepping closer to the bed and taking out my stethoscope to listen to his chest. He was better. We were treating him for pneumonia, and he was improving. I would end my day with a clinical success, however transient and fragile.

As I returned to the nursing station Dolores emerged from the medication room and immediately turned the corner into the south corridor. I hadn't noticed before what excellent posture she had. Mrs. Pierre was back at the desk. I took my charts and sat down behind the counter, and there was Dolores hunched over a chart in her lap, talking on the phone.

"How did she get here? I just saw her walk out of the med room," I said to Mrs. Pierre.

"You must have seen Peggy," she said. We both looked at each other uncertainly, since Dolores was white and Peggy black. I stood up and leaned over the counter to peer down the south corridor. A figure in a white nurse's uniform was rapidly receding from view, slipping past the door at the far end of the corridor.

"Tell the nurses to check the narcotics box," I said to Mrs. Pierre, and I sprang out of the nursing station and took off down the south corridor.

The door at the end of the south corridor of Schilling Three led to the north corridor of Trilling Four. This was a consequence of the law that hospitals must perpetually be under construction so that buildings may end up being erected in different geological eras. I flung open the door and confronted a dilemma. The corridor immediately bifurcated into two arms, the right leading in a straight line to Trilling Four, a surgical floor, and the left twisting around like a maze leading eventually to the Thompson Research Pavilion. If I were her, I would have taken the right branch, with the possibility of ducking into a patient room to hide, rather than risk being overtaken in the maze. I started at the room nearest the door and wove my way in and out, up the corridor, but she had escaped.

When I finished my fruitless search, I walked back to Schilling Three and found Mrs. Stevens, the night shift nursing supervisor, conferring with Peggy and Dolores in the medication room. Most unfortunately, Dolores had left the keys on the counter when she rushed to check on Mrs. Portense and Mrs. Sullivan. The narcotics box had indeed been opened, and two vials of morphine were unaccounted for. The keys had been put back where they were found.

Mrs. Stevens asked me what I had seen and I told her. As we were talking, Mrs. Pierre opened the medication room door to tell Mrs. Stevens that Dr. Thurman was on the phone, returning her call. Dr. Thurman, confusingly, was really a nurse with the title of vice president of patient care services, or some such. Mrs. Stevens scowled, which seemed to me the appropriate response to a call from an upper link of the hospital food chain, but I was surprised that she felt that way, too. The rest of us followed her to the nursing station, and stood listening as she reported the narcotics theft. Dolores and Peggy were promptly distracted, though, by the bombardment of patient calls still bouncing off Mrs. Pierre's console. Mrs. Stevens asked Dr. Thurman if she would like to speak with me, and predictably she said no. I wasn't a nurse, and was probably, in her estimation, too low in the hospital doctor hierarchy for her to be seen associating with, even by telephone.

Mrs. Stevens hung up the phone and said, "If they had any brains they'd call the police."

I asked what would happen next, and she said Dr. Thurman would call Mr. Irnings and they would continue their Mickey Mouse—to use her term—investigation.

"Sounds good," I said.

Dolores, who was back at the nursing station filling out a pharmacy requisition, said softly, to no one in particular, "You mean she'll roll over in bed and tell Mr. Irnings." A wry smile lit fleetingly on Mrs. Steven's face.

I was amazed by Dolores' comment, but then I was always the last to know the good gossip. It wasn't until my third year of residency that I figured out that Dr. Phillips the gastroenterologist and Dr. Phillips the radiologist were married, to each other.

Mrs. Stevens' pager started to beep. She pulled it out of her white coat pocket, squinted at it, and muttered, "CCU." She told Dolores that Dr. Thurman made a point of saying she had to be reprimanded for forgetting the keys. Dolores, who had already expressed her remorse, looked like she was going to cry. "I'll put in the incident report that we talked about the seriousness of this mistake, as we did, and what you will do to avoid making it again, and that should be it," Mrs. Stevens said.

Dolores nodded without looking up and murmured, "Thank you, Mrs. Stevens." She got up to put the pharmacy requisition in the pneumatic tube at the other end of the nursing station.

"It was a bad mistake," Mrs. Stevens said to me, "but I don't know what they expect, having two nurses taking care of 34 patients." I agreed, and she hustled off to stamp out the next fire.

Peggy's voice crackled over the intercom, asking Mrs. Pierre to page the intern on call to come look at Mrs. Downey in fifteen. I had forgotten about Mrs. Downey. I jumped up for the second time and ran, now down the north corridor, to room fifteen. When I got there Peggy was stooping over the bed, listening to the patient's chest with her stethoscope. She straightened up, took out the ear pieces, and asked me if I knew whether Dr. Fabricant was still around. Mrs. Downey was complaining of substernal chest pain. My impulse was to look under the bed to see if Leon was there, and I went so far as to sidestep toward the bathroom so I could make sure it was empty. The patient actually looked pretty chipper. Peggy was asking her to assign a number to the pain, on a scale from one to ten, according to a pain initiative the hospital was aggressively promoting. She pointed to the bulletin board on the wall, where there were pictures of smiley and frowny faces over a row of numbers. Mrs. Downey had to locate her eyeglasses on the bedside stand before she could look at the bulletin board. Like many other patients, she was having difficulty with the number system. It was a five, or maybe more of a three or a four, she didn't want to exaggerate, well, maybe a five after all, no now it was more like a four and a half. Meanwhile the intern arrived, having been across the hall evaluating the patient we had previously found on the floor. He was surprised, but not ungrateful, to find an attending doctor in the room. An EKG machine was hooked up, and the intern and I watched with satisfaction as the tracing emerged, looking normal. He ordered antacids, and a few minutes later the patient announced that she felt much better. I left the intern at the bedside and returned to the nursing station to write my notes.

Before I left the floor, I peeked in room fifteen where Mildred Downey appeared to be resting comfortably, watching television. I took the elevator to the first floor, and cut across a corner of the atrium to the lobby. Out of the corner of my eye I saw a figure flitting past the coffee shop, in the direction of the Doctors' Lounge. I bounded across the atrium to get closer, and I'm sure my jaw dropped open.

"Celine!" I said.

"Oh, hi, Nora."

"Where are you going?"

"I'm covering the psych ER and they called me in to evaluate someone."

I couldn't remember ever seeing a psychiatry attending coming in to the hospital at night for anything, ever. But I had also never worked in the psychiatric emergency department, so maybe it was possible. I wondered who was taking care of the twins, and was just about to ask, when I considered it might be the better part of valor not to mention that I had recently seen Frank. Anyway, it had to be Frank's mother who lived in Queens and always helped them out in emergencies. "Well, I've got to run, I'll talk to you later," Celine said, rushing off.

I walked back across the atrium to the main entrance, wondering who else was prowling around the hospital in the middle of the night. Outside, I navigated the usual pedestrian traffic that was moving in and out of the open food stores and restaurants, the Syrian delicatessen, Cheryl-Lynn's fried chicken, the Szechuan Seventh Heaven, the Cuban anti-Castro liquor store, the organic pastry shop and the Korean market.

When I got home I poured another modest Scotch and lay down on the sofa to think. Why was Leon Fabricant Mildred Downey's doctor? It didn't make sense. I mentally reviewed my list, which was shorter than Aunt Selma's, consisting only of herself, Dr. Townsend, Dr. Pomerantz, the late urologist, and Nurse Eichling. The other names on her list, whoever they were, could be in grave danger.

I went over them again in my head. A few were made up, and a few were from a different era, the decades of Aunt Selma's prime. Someone who had known her in the past could help me, but whom could I approach? Uncle Louie was out of the question. Nor could I imagine confronting Aunt Tootsie.

That settled it.

CHAPTER ELEVEN

It was early afternoon on a raw day in late February when I arrived at Union Station in New Haven. My cousin Scott had supplied me with the address of the Vista View Rest Home and had phoned the proprietor, a Mrs. Beazley, in advance of my visit. I stepped into a taxi outside the station and rode to 143 Lombard Avenue. Situated between two larger thoroughfares, my destination turned out to be a narrow residential block lined on both sides with cars parked bumper to bumper. As I had expected, the view was no great shakes. Number 143 was a rambling wood and brick Victorian-era house, with multiple additions, that sprawled across two lots. It wasn't dilapidated, although I wouldn't have called it spiffy either. There was a light cover of snow on Lombard Avenue that gave way to a gritty admixture of ice and sand on the sidewalk and walkway leading to the front steps of Vista View. As the cab drove away I lingered at the curb, looking up and down the street. The neighboring houses were also built on a large scale. They had probably been one-family dwellings in their heyday but were now chopped up into apartments, judging from the multiple mailboxes tacked up at each front door. Some, like the one I hesitant to enter, had their yards torn up to make tiny parking lots.

I walked up the soggy wooden steps to the front door and rang the bell. A woman's voice over an intercom asked who I was. I gave my name and said I was expected. The door buzzed open, and I entered a huge, unfurnished square foyer, and came face to face with a slight, gray-haired woman in a jogging outfit with food stains on the sweatshirt. "Angie!" she cried.

"No, it's not Angie," a voice called from around a corner. Another woman, wearing a pink nurse's aide uniform, and considerably younger, appeared and steered the older woman in the direction of another large, open room to our left. "I'll be right with you," she called to me over her shoulder.

"I think that's Angie," the older woman protested as she was dropped on a sofa.

The nurse's aide returned, and said, "You've come to see Bella, right?"

I winced, as I always do at the common health care industry practice of calling elderly people by their first names, but I wasn't going to argue with my connection.

"That's right," I said. "She knows, doesn't she?"

"Oh, yes, and I reminded her this morning."

With that, she crossed the foyer and ascended a staircase that carried her out of view. Meanwhile, Angie's friend jumped up from the sofa and wandered back to the foyer where she stood a millimeter from me, breathing heavily. We waited there, together, for a long time. Twice I heard footsteps overhead, but no one appeared. A television could be heard in the distance, along with muffled voices, and I surmised there was some kind of recreation room somewhere. Finally, the nurse's aide returned, leading a tall, thin, stooped figure with white-streaked jet-black hair, high cheekbones, and mustard-colored skin.

I watched as they progressed laboriously down the stairs. "Caroline, stay away from Miss Sternberg!" the nurse's aide snapped at my companion. Aunt Bunny halted at the sound of her name, and her guide pulled her forward, saying in a sing-song voice, "Your niece is Miss Sternberg, too."

At this, Aunt Bunny looked not only bewildered but steamed, and had to be coaxed down the remaining stairs. Finally they landed, and pulling her by the arm, the nurse's aid maneuvered Aunt Bunny across the foyer to the large room. I followed, Caroline shuffling to keep up with me. Aunt Bunny, who had apparently decided not to look at me, was settled into an armchair, and I moved a second chair over to sit facing her. I thanked the nurse's aide and asked her name. "Just call me Brenda," she said. Brenda took Caroline's hand and told her they were going back to the television room. Without another glance at me, the older woman let Brenda lead her away.

Aunt Bunny and I now sat alone. I couldn't remember when I had ever felt more awkward. She stared at the floor with the flat, self-absorbed expression of schizophrenics who are well medicated, and I realized she wasn't going to say anything voluntarily.

"You know who I am, Aunt Bunny, don't you?"

She didn't look up.

"I'm Harry Sternberg's granddaughter. My parents were Arthur and Teddy Sternberg." I could hear myself enunciating very slowly, as if to a non-English speaker.

Still no response.

I decided I might as well lay it on her. "I've brought bad news," I said. With that, she looked at me but remained silent, and I thought, what if she's mute?

She looked down at the floor again. Like Aunt Selma she had large gray eyes, but hers seemed to be fixed wide open. I wondered if anyone had checked her thyroid.

"Aunt Selma, your sister Selma, has died," I said. I moved up in my chair, close enough to touch her. Still staring at the floor, she rotated one ankle back and forth, and I noticed, with a jolt, that she was wearing orthopedic shoes. Then she uttered her first word.

"Where?" she asked.

Of all possible questions, this seemed a bizarre choice. "At Lafayette Medical Center," I answered.

She leaned forward and glanced at the empty space to her right, then back at the floor. Her foot was now oscillating rapidly. She said, "She should have told the truth."

I was stunned. "The truth? What do you mean the truth?"

Aunt Bunny sank back in the armchair, as if worn out from conversation. Her gaze settled on a distant point beyond my shoulder. Although I knew no one was there, I couldn't stop myself from turning and looking at the empty foyer.

"Aunt Bunny," I persisted, "The truth about what?"

No answer. She seemed to be involuting in front of me, and I started to panic. Rising from my chair, I leaned over her and tapped forcefully on her thin shoulder. "Aunt Bunny, please!" I nearly shouted in her ear.

"Ouch!" she said, grabbing her shoulder, "Don't do that!" I had gotten her attention. She regarded me angrily as I resumed my seat, and after a long pause, said, "I forgot whose daughter you are."

"Arthur and Theodora's. My grandfather was Harry Sternberg."

She nodded but looked over my head.

"What do you mean, 'She should have told the truth'?" I persisted.

Now she was eyeing my feet, and despite myself I felt impelled to look at them. I had on black leather boots, and they looked fine.

I was debating whether I'd have to get up and shake her again when she asked, still looking away from me, "Did she have an operation?"

"How did you know that?"

She shifted a few inches forward in her chair and whispered, "On her brain?" Aunt Bunny was leaning toward me, her mouth slightly open. She clenched the arms of her chair with her spidery hands and fixed me with an eerie intensity bordering on creepiness.

"Her brain?" I whispered back. I felt my spine press against the back of my chair. She continued to watch me expectantly. Yep, that's why she's here, I told myself, because she's psycho. She's the crazy one, but I'm OK, I'm only visiting. Yet I had the unsettling premonition, sitting alone with Aunt Bunny in that cavernous room, that my sanity was a fleeting thing. It was just a matter of time until I was packed off to a rest home to sit in a chair in orthopedic shoes and ask tangential questions in the vein of my ancestors. I had to remember to tell Brad to shoot me first.

"No, it was on her hip," I mumbled.

"The right hip?"

My God, there was no end to her weirdness. "No, it was the left hip, actually," I said. "Does it matter?"

She looked down and pursed her lips tightly, and for a moment I thought she might spit on the floor.

"I expected it," she said.

"You expected her to break her hip?"

"Can't believe it," she muttered, as if to herself. I wasn't sure if she had heard me or not. "She was never afraid of anything." That was the truth, as far as I knew, but I didn't see how it related to our topic.

In fact, I was completely thrown off by her responses. All the way to New Haven I had rehearsed the questions that I would ask her and had imagined, with boundless naiveté, how she might answer. Now the idea that I would be able to glean anything useful from her seemed ridiculous. I was probably lucky that she recognized my parents' names. I didn't have much hope, but I decided to give it one more shot.

"Is there anything you can tell me that would help me understand Aunt Selma's death?" I asked her. She was studying the blunted tip of her orthopedic shoe, and I realized it was impossible to determine how much of what I said penetrated. For all I knew, there could have been a whole congress of other voices in the room competing for her attention.

"They were on the wrong side," she said.

"Who was?"

"All of them." She was twisting her foot again, this way and that.

For a minute or two we both sat in silence. In my mind I castigated myself for wasting most of a day traveling to Connecticut to interrogate a psychotic person. What went on in Aunt Bunny's mind was anyone's guess. Every so often she looked to her left or right. The situation was maddening, yet it was impossible to resent her. On the contrary, sitting across from her as she receded into her thin, dark, defiant Sternbergness, I realized with dismay that I liked her.

Finally I said, "Aunt Bunny, I don't know what you're talking about."

"Oh," she answered, looking down at her hands folded in her lap.

"I have to go back to New York."

She didn't react.

"How do I get Brenda?" She pointed to a square metal box on the end table by the sofa. I pressed the button in its center, and after a minute or so, during which Aunt Bunny and I continued communing with our own thoughts, Brenda joined us from somewhere beyond the foyer. She helped Aunt Bunny out of her armchair and walked her back in the direction of the staircase. I stood still, watching their slow progress, then caught up with them in three strides and asked

Aunt Bunny, "Who looks after you, who helps you?" She stared at me, apparently not comprehending.

Brenda replied, in a soothing voice, "Mrs. Beazely and I take care of them, and the visiting nurses, and Dr. Lemon." Mrs. Beazely was out at the moment. Dr. Lemon was the psychiatrist. I asked about a medical doctor, and Brenda said they all had their own private doctors. She could look up the name of my aunt's doctor if I wanted. I said I would find out later.

I stepped closer to Aunt Bunny and said, "Is there anything I can do for you, Aunt Bunny?"

In a bland voice she said simply, "No," and continued her snail's pace toward her room. Brenda, looking over her shoulder at me while continuing to guide Aunt Bunny, said I could use the phone in the foyer if I needed to call a cab.

Anxious to escape Vista View Rest Home, I waited for the taxi outside. The sky had become overcast, and a brisk wind was blowing a few snowflakes around. Lombard Avenue was preternaturally quiet. I wondered what sequence of events and decisions had landed Aunt Bunny in this unlikely place, and I suspected that the one person who could have told me the whole story was Aunt Selma. We had only had a million conversations in which she could have shared some of this information with me. Scott obviously knew much more than I, but he probably wouldn't feel at liberty to divulge it. Well, I'd ask him anyway. I had to talk to him about Aunt Bunny's care. She should have been spending more time with other people, not sequestered in her room.

On the return trip to New York I tried to distract myself with the *Times* crossword puzzle, until somewhere near Stamford I gave up. I remembered the photograph of Aunt Bunny and my mother, and having thought of it I couldn't get it out of my mind. My mother had been able to put her arm around Aunt Bunny, but I had been deflected by her delusional field, like one magnet to another. Just thinking about it wore me out, and soon I closed my eyes and fell asleep. I dreamed I was at my parents' house, standing in the doorway to the garage. A black sedan slowly pulled into the garage, and as it approached I saw that the driver was my mother, looking like she did in photographs taken when she was in her thirties. Sitting in the middle of the back seat was a little girl in a party dress. When the car came to a stop I saw that it was a hearse. I hate that dream.

I awoke as the train pulled into Grand Central Station. It was almost four-thirty, and it would have been perfectly reasonable to go home. Instead, I rode the subway to the hospital.

I headed straight for the atrium coffee shop, which was almost empty, bought a cup of coffee, and used a house phone to page Andy Redman, one of my PCIMC colleagues, who had covered me for the day on Schilling Three. He was in his office in clinic.

"You didn't have to come back to the hospital," he said.

"I know, but here I am," I sighed. "Do you want to give me the sign-out for tomorrow?"

"Sure," he said. "You want it over the phone, or do you want to meet me?"

"The phone's OK." I pulled up a chair from an adjacent atrium table.

"Just let me get my list."

I heard papers rustling. "Take your time."

"OK. Delacruz, nothing really, got a central line for TPN." By that he meant total parenteral nutrition. "Abbot, got his thoracentesis."

"Who did it?"

"Michelle."

"Good."

"And it looks like a transudate. Slobodian, oh, there were problems with him. Cultures came back positive for *Pseudomonas*."

"Yikes."

"Yeah, and his creatinine went up to six. Renal said they'll probably dialyze him tomorrow, and there's no space, so we moved him to the ICU."

"How's his pressure been?"

"OK. A little high, actually. They have to take fluid off. Monroe, asthma's about the same. We continued the IV steroids. Lewis, started to withdraw, really shaky, I was worried about DT's. Anyway, we upped the Librium, and he's better."

"I knew it," I muttered.

"Rivera, had his cath, clean coronaries, home tomorrow. Let's see, French, nothing, awaiting placement." This was a term I hated, though we all used it, and it was probably the most honest description of what it represented: admission to a nursing home. "Dumont, Surgery came by and decided he should stay on our service."

"Give me a break."

"Yeah, really."

"So now we're treating cholecystitis? Who's the attending?"

"Daines."

"OK, I'll call him tomorrow."

"Reyes, totally confused on rounds this morning, thought she was at the beauty parlor. Probably has to do with her meds, so we're holding almost everything. And I think that's it."

"Thanks, Andy, let me know when I can pay you back," I said.

"Well, I'm on service in July," he said. July was the month that the new interns arrived.

After I hung up I called Schilling Three, and sure enough Paul was there with the rest of our team.

"We're on our way to Pathology," he told me. "The biopsy slides on Armstrong are out." Renee Armstrong was a patient on our service with kidney disease who had undergone a renal biopsy two days before. I figured I might as well go along and told Paul I would meet them in the Pathology Department.

As usual, I had to roam the confusing corridors of the sub-basement before I found my destination. This time it was the office of Walter Fish, and as I approached it I remembered with a pang our last meeting. The door was open so I entered and discovered that my team had preceded me. Paul, Michelle, Roman, Tonya and Patrick were lined up at the row of teaching microscopes that were connected to each other and to the one commanded by Dr. Fish. They all had their heads bent as they peered into their respective eyepieces.

"Hello, Nora," Dr. Fish said, looking up momentarily. "How are you doing?"

"All right," I said.

"Good. It's nice to see you. This is a good case." He redirected his monocular attention to the microscope, holding his eyeglasses in one hand and steering with the other. "See the glomerulus near the top of the slide? My eleven o'clock. Everyone got it?" He paused a minute so everyone could get oriented. "Now look at it under high power." He flipped the lenses on his microscope. "Nice thin, delicate capillary loops. It's normal, right?" He crossed to another part of the slide, navigating his way through the kidney tissue. "Meanwhile, in the interstitium we see an inflammatory infiltrate. Right here, for instance, all the mononuclear cells—lymphocytes and plasma cells. What—ho! What's this?" He stopped short. "Well?"

No one said anything.

"Right in the middle of the slide," Dr. Fish prompted.

"A white cell cast in a tubule," Roman said, apparently correctly.

"Where?" Patrick asked.

"My four o'clock. See it?" Dr. Fish said.

"Here, Dr. Sternberg, have a look," Paul said, stepping back so I could use his microscope.

I adjusted the eyepieces and said, "You mean ten o'clock."

"No, no," the pathologist corrected me. "Remember the images are flipped. I've got it at four o'clock, so you see it at ten. And what's this here?"

There didn't seem to be any takers, then Tonya hazarded, "The tubular membrane's disrupted."

"Very good. It's being invaded by a lymphocyte." Dr. Fish looked up to see who had answered and Tonya immediately looked down. Couldn't deal with the game eye.

We sailed around the slide a little more, Dr. Fish enthusiastically pointing out the sights of interest. Our tour probably would have lasted longer except that his secretary interrupted to remind him he had a department meeting. He grimaced, and we pushed back from our microscopes and thanked him.

"Thank *you*," he said. "Interesting case."

As we left his office and reassembled in the corridor Patrick asked, "So the diagnosis is acute interstitial nephritis?"

"That's it," Roman said. "Most likely from her antibiotics."

"Did you stop them?" Paul asked him.

Roman nodded. "And the Renal fellow told me to start steroids this morning."

"You should check with the nurses before you leave and make sure they've picked up the orders and there's no problem," Paul said. He then reminded me that it was our admitting day. "There are already four hits, I mean admissions, in the ER," he said. I told them to go do their work, and we dispersed.

Retracing my steps, I turned left into another tunnel and glimpsed Roberta Garrett walking briskly about thirty feet ahead of me, not that surprising, I guess, since I was in her territory. At the sight of her I felt suddenly claustrophobic. She vanished around a bend in the corridor, and I beat it for the stairway that led to the atrium. Barely pausing for air, I plowed straight home.

There was a message on the machine from Jessica, wanting

to know how I had made out in New Haven. I heard a toy drum pounding in the background so I inferred she was home. When I called back she put the phone on speaker mode and shouted, "Do you mind if I change Drew's diaper while we talk?"

"Not at all," I replied. "There's not much to say. It was a bust."

"Thank you, Frieda, that's beautiful. Did you color it yourself? With Miss Diana? Wow, that's great. Don't pinch him, darling."

I could hear Drew starting to cry.

"Why?" Jessica asked.

"She's totally psychotic. I don't know what I was expecting."

"Frieda, don't pinch him. So she couldn't tell you anything?"

"I'm not pinching him."

"Yes, I think you are, sweetie." Drew was now shrieking. "He doesn't want you to do that. Frieda!"

Frieda let out a horrible scream, followed by loud sobbing. "He kicked me!"

"Maybe I should let you go," I suggested.

"DO NOT KICK HIM. Yeah, I'm sorry. I'll have to talk to you tomorrow."

"Goodbye Frieda, goodbye Drew," I called out.

Frieda stopped crying abruptly and answered, in a tiny voice, "Bye, Nora."

CHAPTER TWELVE

The next morning I was back at the hospital at 7:15 for Grand Rounds. As the name implies, this is the big event of the week for the department of medicine. Everyone makes an appearance: Lafayette faculty, housestaff, and third and fourth year medical students, private physicians from the community, the Medicine faculty and housestaff from Saint Stephen's Hospital, the community hospital about twenty blocks south, and internists from the local clinics. I arrived just in time to join the logjam of white coats outside the Schaeffer Amphitheater, crowding in to sign the attendance sheet at the door.

Inside, I climbed to the back of the amphitheater and took an aisle seat near one of the exits. It was always a good idea to have an escape route in case the lecture turned deadly. I looked around for Jessica but didn't see her, though I spotted my team a few rows in front of me to the right, guzzling coffee. The Saint Stephen's crowd was sitting behind them, their Chief of Medicine, Hank Zurich, and associate chief, Brendan Waterhouse, both formerly on the staff of

Lafayette, with a few other attendings and a group of their residents. They always looked authentically collegial. Brendan was waving at Eugene Velazquez, my former medical school classmate and fellow resident, who was ascending the stairs two at a time. Eugene worked at the Van Dyke West Side Community Health Center, the independent, non-profit clinic that survived on the edge of insolvency in the shadow of the Medical Center. Van Dyke catered to the same clientele as the Medical Center; I imagined some patients chose to be seen at PCIMC because of Lafayette's reputation while others stuck with Van Dyke because of its graduated fee-scale for the uninsured. Eugene had gone there to work right after residency, the same time I had started at PCIMC. Because the Van Dyke doctors admitted their patients to Lafayette, we tended to see each other frequently around the hospital. As Eugene sat down next to me I noticed his face was sunburned and his wavy black hair a little longer than usual.

"Where were you?" I asked.

"Puerto Rico. Visited my grandfather." He took off his suede bomber jacket and flattened it against the back of his seat. "How are you?" Eugene regarded me intently, and I knew he was alluding to Aunt Selma.

"OK, more or less," I said.

He changed the subject and asked if the hospital's missing narcotics had been found.

"You've heard about that?"

He shrugged. "I think everyone has."

"Well that's ironic," I said, "since the hospital's trying to keep it a big secret."

"That's a bad strategy." Eugene stretched his legs as much as he could in the cramped seat. "Though not surprising, I guess." He spread his hands out in front of him, and I tried, as always, not to stare at them. They were large, square and perfectly proportioned with long, graceful fingers. I had been fascinated by his hands ever since we worked on the same cadaver in anatomy class, the dissection groups being assigned alphabetically.

"Where's Brad these days?" he asked.

"In Norway."

I glimpsed Jessica threading her way through a crowded row near the front of the amphitheater where her husband Ray was sitting, and waved to her, but she was engrossed in a conversation with one of the endocrinology fellows.

Eugene followed my line of vision and said, "I saw Jess last weekend at the diabetes fair."

"I know. She told me."

"Do you want to have dinner tonight?"

"Oh, I can't Eugene," I said. "I was out of the hospital yesterday and there were at least four admissions. I have too much to catch up on."

Wally Todd was approaching the lectern to introduce the speaker, Myron Lattimore from the division of hematology and oncology. He was one of my most boring professors in medical school. Meanwhile the first slide appeared on the screen behind him, announcing his topic: "The Coagulation Disorders: Through Thick and Thin."

"Oh boy, we're in for it," I said. Eugene smiled. Wally was delivering his usual stiff introduction, reciting excerpts from

Myron's curriculum vitae which he punctuated with flashes of his signature humorless smile. Myron took the podium, and adhering to the traditional formula of Grand Rounds, opened with a case presentation. This was succeeded by a lecture with the inevitable slide presentation. I wondered how Grand Rounds had ever been conducted before the invention of the slide projector, like in the days of Dr. Osler, not to mention Galen. I supposed the speakers displayed organs from the autopsies that house officers and senior doctors were always running down to the basement to perform.

Myron spoke in a relentlessly nasal monotone that could have desiccated the juiciest subject. As he droned on about coagulation factors I tried to make up my mind between napping and slipping out the exit. When I was a resident I would, on such occasions, stealthily activate my beeper then affect disgusted resignation as I walked out to answer my fake call. But I didn't think that was appropriate behavior for an attending. The third option was to try and hang on to the ladder of clotting factors now being projected on the screen, but it slithered out of my grasp. I dozed on and off for the rest of the hour and was finally awakened by the applause. Wally strode back to the podium to begin the obligatory esoteric questions and answers, after which we were released.

Rather than duck out the near exit, I made my way down the stairs, Eugene behind me, to catch up with Jessica. We overtook her in the white-coated phalanx advancing up the corridor toward the front door of the North Building, right across the street from the main entrance to the hospital. Jessica asked Eugene if he was going to Griffin Garrett's dinner, and he replied in the negative.

"Oh, come on," Jessica wailed. "Are Ray and I going to have to sit by ourselves? Nora won't come because Brad'll be in Hong Kong."

"That's not why I'm not going."

"I'll go with you," Eugene said to me.

Jessica squeezed his arm. "That's great! We'll all sit together, it'll be fun."

"It won't be fun," I scowled, "and honestly I don't want to listen to speeches about what a sterling guy Griffin Garrett was—is. But thank you, Eugene."

We exited the North Building with the rest of the throng and rushed across the street, heads down and coats pulled in tightly against the cold air. Jessica asked Eugene if he had time to join us for coffee in the atrium, but he said he had to get back to Van Dyke.

"Call me if you change your mind, Nora," he said as he stepped into the wind, heading in the direction of the parking garage. Jessica and I waved to him and hurried through the revolving doors.

We bought coffee and sat down in the atrium at the table nearest to the waterfall. Jessica commented that it was a shame my meeting with Aunt Bunny hadn't yielded anything.

"It was silly of me to think it would," I said.

"What's your aunt's diagnosis?"

I shrugged. "Who knows. Some type of schizophrenia."

"Is she on antipsychotics?"

"Oh, yeah, for many years, I'm sure."

"Have you talked to Celine about her?"

It was a logical question, and I realized that I hadn't brought up Aunt Bunny with Celine because, for one reason, Celine and I had

had more pressing matters to discuss.

"I guess—Look," Jessica interrupted herself, "There's Margaret Van Horne." She nodded in the direction of our former Pediatrics professor who was dashing across the atrium toward the South Building elevators.

"Wow, I don't think I've seen her in over a year," I said.

"You could see her every month if you attended medical staff meetings."

"Come on, Department of Medicine meetings are painful enough," I answered defensively. "Anyway, I read the minutes."

"Doesn't she look great?" Jessica asked rhetorically.

To us, she always looked great. Margaret was legendary among the women doctors of Lafayette who had been her students. Tall and harmoniously oversized with a big frame and big blonde hair, she rattled by on three-inch heels. She wore a striped knit top and rose-colored skirt under her big white coat. As usual, her eyelids were made up with colorful eye shadow, and her lashes were matted with mascara. Margaret had gone to medical school when there was only a handful of women in each class, smaller even than the fifteen percent of my class who were women. She had married one of her classmates, Edward Van Horne, a cardiologist, and given birth to their first two children while she was still in medical school, the third and fourth during residency, and the fifth shortly after joining the faculty of the Department of Pediatrics. When lecturing medical students, she liked to keep the audience awake with little asides describing the reaction of senior attendings whenever she arrived for work at the hospital noticeably pregnant. Jessica maintained that it was disingenuous of her not to state publicly that, as Jessica put it, "When they told us 'You can have it all,' they were lying," or to acknowledge that she was able to pull it off because she and her husband made a lot of money. But I wondered whether admitting the difficulties of simultaneously being a full-time physician, wife, and mother was a luxury that the women doctors of her generation thought they couldn't afford.

Margaret caught sight of us and detoured full-speed to our table. "How are you both? Nora, I haven't seen you in a long time," she said.

I leaned back to grab another chair and drag it over, but Margaret stopped me with a flutter of her hand. "I can't stay. Ed's in the GI Suite having a polyp removed, and I want to see how he's doing." I couldn't imagine Ed would be happy knowing Margaret was discussing his colon. "Jessica, seeing you here reminded me, I want to put something on the next medical staff meeting agenda." She suddenly looked perplexed and said, "But why am I telling you? I'll call Bill Shell's secretary."

"Thank you, Margaret," Jessica said, casting me a smug look.

"I'll give you a preview anyway. Ed's retiring in June."

"Retiring?" we echoed. This was surprising news, since Ed couldn't have been much more than fifty.

"Well, retiring from medicine, I should say. He's going to run for Congress."

I guess our jaws dropped open because Margaret burst into her rippling, soprano laugh and said, "That's how everyone responds."

"It's so unexpected," Jessica said. "I had no idea Ed was interested in politics."

"He's considered running for office for a long time. I think the latest round of productivity standards finally pushed him over the edge. Of course, it scares me to death." She didn't look scared at all. "When Freddy was born we had that Romanian nanny who insisted on being paid in cash."

"That's right, they're going to look into all that stuff," Jessica concurred.

"Where is he running?" I asked.

"In Westchester," Margaret said. "First he has to win the primary." I was tempted to ask which party but decided it was safer not to inquire. I didn't vote in Westchester, anyway. Then I had an alarming thought.

"Margaret, is Ed telling people he's retiring?" I asked. "I mean, do you think he'd mention it to anyone in the GI suite?"

She looked at me quizzically. "Probably not. He doesn't use the word 'retirement.'"

"Oh, that's wonderful," I said, relieved.

"Why?" Margaret asked. "I don't follow you."

Jessica tried to help me out. "Well, he's embarking on a new career," she added. "You want to accentuate the positive."

"So I wouldn't say anything about retiring from medicine," I advised her. "It sounds so negative."

"It does? I don't think so."

"Tell Ed good luck," Jessica said.

"All right, I will. Good to see you both," Margaret said, and we watched her tap away like a mad castanet in her stiletto pumps.

I swallowed the rest of my coffee and said, "I've got to go, too, or I'll be late for rounds."

"I'll go with you as far as the ballroom," Jessica said as we got up from the table and pushed in our chairs. "You don't think Ed's at any risk, do you?"

"Not as long as he keeps his mouth shut," I said. "They must have him well-sedated for the procedure."

"Isn't this horrible? Listen to us. We're worried that every retired doctor's at risk of being bumped off."

We crossed the atrium heading toward the corridor that led to the South Building elevators. The stretch of wall where the hallway curved, alongside the lobby, served as a miniature gallery displaying objects and photographs pertaining to Lafayette historical themes, probably selected by the Ladies' Auxiliary or a similar group. As we walked by I noticed that a new exhibit had been mounted. I habitually checked out these exhibits on my way to Schilling Three, and I hadn't seen this one previously, so it must have just gone up. It featured enlarged grainy, dark, photographs of masked and gowned surgeons and nurses huddled over operating tables, followed by similar pictures of white-coated pathologists bent over microscopes. Hung next to the latter was a blow-up of a pathology slide. Looking at it, I remembered my disorientation in Walter Fish's laboratory the day before. I had forgotten that the images under the multiheaded microscope were reversed, as in a mirror. You had to mentally translocate the right and left, and north and south sides of the image. I had looked at the wrong side. So, big deal, I thought. Why did this bother me? It wasn't such a horrible mistake. I was on the wrong side. Right.

I stopped short in front of the exhibit, and Jessica said, "I don't have a lot of time, Nora."

Did they operate on the right hip? No, I told her, it was the left hip. But what if she meant something entirely different? What if she meant: was it the wrong hip? *They were on the wrong side.*

"Oh my God," I said out loud.

"What? What?" Jessica asked.

"I have to go back to New Haven. I—I have to go right now."

"What happened? What's going on?" We stood staring at each other. She grabbed my arm and gave it a good yank. "Tell me what's going on!"

I shook my head. "It's too complicated. I'm not sure yet." I hurried toward the house phone on the wall behind us. "I have to call Andy and see if he can cover me again."

"I'll ask him," Jessica said.

I held the receiver in mid-air. "What if he can't do it?"

"Then I'll do it."

"Are you sure?"

"Yeah. Don't worry. Just call me when you get back."

I replaced the phone. "We start rounds on the north corridor—"

"Don't worry, I'll page Paul—isn't he your resident?"

"Yeah. He knows everything about the patients. There are some new admissions, though. I don't know how many."

"Nora, just go. Paul and I will figure it out."

"Thanks." I leaned forward and kissed her cheek, which I don't think I had ever done before, and sped through the lobby to the Doctors' Lounge. I hung up my white coat in the cloak room, grabbed my winter coat, and raced back outside. I could see the shuttle way up the street, lumbering in traffic toward the hospital. No time to wait. I ran southward to the subway stop, flew down the stairs and rode to Times Square, then across to Grand Central Station. I had fifteen minutes before the next train left for New Haven, so I went to a phone and called Scott's office in Metuchen.

Scott was in court and would be there all day, his secretary told me. I asked if she could call ahead to Vista View Rest Home and alert them that I was returning for another visit with Aunt Bunny. After that I bought a copy of the *Times*, which was a little extravagant since we had it delivered, but I would need the crossword on the train to occupy my mind.

Within two hours I was face to face with Brenda again. The set up was identical to the day before, the vacant sitting room, the low background noise of canned laughter from an unseen television, with the exception that my greeter, Angie's pal, was missing. Brenda climbed the stairs to fetch Aunt Bunny, but instead of cooling my heels in the foyer, I sat down in an armchair in the large room, then jumped up, then sat down again, then paced around the chair as I waited.

After about fifteen minutes Aunt Bunny appeared, plodding across the foyer with Brenda. As at the start of our last visit, she stared at the floor while Brenda helped her settle in a chair. She was wearing a different outfit, a brown and tan houndstooth print dress with a pointed collar, four-button placket, and a narrow belt of the same fabric, probably rayon. The hem hit two inches below the knee. She had worn a very similar dress the previous day, but in a solid brown. Both were well kept, and she might have owned them for one month or twenty years. I wondered who helped her dress, who bought her clothes.

I sat down again, pulled my chair closer to hers and said, "Aunt Bunny, I hope you don't mind my coming back to see you so soon."

Her head was bent, and she didn't answer me.

"I realized that when I was here yesterday you were trying to tell me something important."

She stared with even greater intensity at her feet. Though I hated myself for doing it, I looked at them, too. She had on those damn orthopedic shoes.

"Aunt Bunny, when you said that Aunt Selma should have told the truth, you were referring to something specific that happened, weren't you?"

She shifted just perceptibly in her chair, head still lowered.

"What did you mean when you said they were on the wrong side?"

No answer.

"The wrong side of what?"

Aunt Bunny shot a glance at the ceiling, then back at the floor, and again I wondered if she was listening to other voices. Whatever she was doing, I was running out of patience. "I know you just met me for the first time yesterday," I said in the most forbearing tone I could muster. "And I know, or at least I'm guessing, that this may be a painful subject. But I'm trying to figure out the—the circumstances of Aunt Selma's death, and I think you're the only person who can help me."

She stooped forward in her chair, head down, so it was impossible for me to see her face. Two can play this game, I thought, and I squatted on the floor in front of her chair. "You know what I think?" I whispered. "I think Aunt Selma screwed something up at the hospital and lied about it."

Her head snapped up, the wide gray eyes even wider and her face tinged red. She snorted, "Not Selma."

I leaned closer to her and said, "Who?"

Aunt Bunny looked away, focusing on her left hand which was clamped to the arm of the chair. I put my hands on top of hers, bent my back lower, and looked up into her face so that she was forced to look at me.

"Stop that!" she said, wriggling her hands in my grasp and trying to pull away from me.

"You better tell me," I hissed. She was panting. "Don't hyperventilate. You'll pass out."

"Whose daughter are you?"

"I'm your brother Harry's granddaughter."

"You're a pain in the neck!"

"Thank you. Who was on the wrong side?"

"Let go of my hands!"

I lifted my hands, releasing hers. "Who was on the wrong side?"

"Sit in your chair." It was amazing. She sounded just like Aunt Selma, and I obeyed. She stared down at her lap, twisting her fingers.

"Well?" I said. "What should Aunt Selma have told the truth about?"

She was bending her head lower again. She certainly had a flexible cervical spine for a person her age. I leaned forward and slowly repeated, "What should Aunt Selma have told the truth about?"

She rocked from side to side, and without looking up, mumbled, "The operation."

I felt an electric shock tingle through me, not unpleasantly, unlike the time I grabbed the rewired lamp in the emergency room to do a pelvic exam and electrocuted myself.

"The brain surgery." She spoke in a flat voice without any modulation.

"What happened in the brain surgery?" I had advanced to the edge of the chair and was tilting toward her, barely breathing.

"They were on the wrong side."

"The wrong side of—the brain?"

She nodded.

"Someone operated on the wrong side of somebody's brain?"

"Yeah."

"How could that happen?"

"She had a cancer, but he took out some other part of her brain."

"Who? Deliberately?" I asked.

She looked at me with what might have been a disgusted smirk, I couldn't tell. "No. It was a mistake."

"Was Aunt Selma involved in the operation?"

She nodded again.

"Maybe she didn't know it was a mistake."

"They all knew," she said.

"Who?"

"Everyone who was in the operation!" She was becoming exasperated with me. "They thought it was a different patient."

"But they didn't say anything, didn't report it, is that it?"

"She covered up for him. And the lady died." It was unnerving to hear such a grisly charge made in a toneless voice.

"Why would Aunt Selma do that?"

"I forgot whose daughter you are."

"Arthur's. Harry's granddaughter."

She paused, then said, "The baby."

The baby? Was she talking about me? Or my grandfather? He wasn't the baby. This was trouble.

"Harry's not the youngest," I corrected her. "Louie's the youngest."

She shook her head. "Charlotte was the baby."

"Charlotte?" I repeated, not comprehending.

"Yeah."

She's totally confused, I thought. That meant the whole thing could be delusional, a confabulation. I didn't know if I could bear it. "Aunt Bunny, do you know who Charlotte is?"

She nodded and said, "Charlotte was Selma's daughter."

"Oh, my God."

She had stopped wringing her hands and was sitting straight in her chair, staring at my shoes.

"Aunt Selma had a daughter?"

No answer.

"Who—who—." My epiglottis was obstructing, but finally I managed to disgorge some air and squeak, "Who was the father?"

"He was."

"He? Who?" Then it registered. "The surgeon?"

She nodded her head. "She said she didn't want to ruin him. So he could support the child."

"But Charlotte is Uncle Oscar's daughter," I said feebly.

"Oscar and his wife took the baby."

"You knew this all the time. That means they all knew it, Aunt Tootsie, Uncle Louie…" She didn't answer me. I said, louder, "Do Aunt Tootsie and Uncle Louie know about this?"

"Louie doesn't know." She was still examining my feet, and I instinctively pulled them in.

"Why not?"

"Too young."

"Does Charlotte know?"

She shook her head.

"What was the name of the surgeon?"

She started twisting her fingers again.

"This is important, Aunt Bunny." I stuck out my hand to take hers, but she recoiled and I withdrew it. "Please, Aunt Bunny."

"Can I tell you?" she whispered.

"Yes."

She grimaced, wrinkling her nose as if contemplating something repulsive, and spat out, "Garrett."

"And the name of the woman, the patient who died?"

But she was spent, rendered speechless after such an extraordinary display of verbosity. Clamping her mouth shut, she collapsed against the back of the chair. She shot a glance at the empty space to her left, frowned, and looked down again. I wondered if her other companions were telling her to zip it.

"Please, Aunt Bunny, you have to tell me." I sprang out of my chair and knelt in front of her.

"I don't know," she mumbled.

"What do you mean you don't know?"

"Selma never told me her name."

I couldn't believe it. "Then why did she tell you about it at all?" I asked, infuriated.

"She felt bad."

"Does Aunt Tootsie know?"

"No."

"No?"

She glanced to the left again and shook her head. "She didn't tell Tootsie about the operation. She only told me."

"She must have loved you a lot." I don't know why I said that. It just spilled out of my mouth. Aunt Bunny, now staring at the floor, didn't react. She tipped her head slightly leftward then right, as if considering both sides of a question. Her face reassumed the distant, preoccupied expression I had observed earlier. She's withdrawing beyond my reach, I thought, and a voracious sadness began to swallow me. No time, I told myself. I had to get back to New York. I had to find, of all people, Griffin Garrett.

I said, "I'm going to call Brenda," and I pressed the button on the metal box by my elbow. Aunt Bunny sat hunched forward, head down. She was thinner than Aunt Selma, but even with her face half hidden they bore, in old age as in youth, an unmistakable resemblance. I wanted to touch her arm, but I was afraid she'd recoil from me again, so we waited together in isolation for the nurse's aide.

When Brenda appeared in the doorway, Aunt Bunny began to stand up unassisted. She had had enough of me. "Did you have a nice chat?" Brenda asked, in her professional, sing-song voice, as she took Aunt Bunny's arm.

"Yes, very nice, thanks," I said mechanically. Again I watched them creep toward the empty foyer and the staircase. "Aunt Bunny, don't you want to stay downstairs, with the other people?" I asked, hesitating behind them.

They kept walking, and Brenda replied, looking at Aunt Bunny rather than me, "Bella likes to spend the afternoons in her room."

Were they incarcerating her, I wondered. I had to remember to call Scott as soon as possible.

"Thank you, Aunt Bunny, you've helped me a lot," I said, again addressing her back. They continued toward the stairs. "Can I use the phone to call New York?" I asked Brenda.

She told me the code to enter for a long-distance call, and I dialed Jessica's beeper number, punched in the Vista View number, and waited. Within five minutes she called back, not long after Aunt Bunny and Brenda reached the top of the stairs and disappeared from view. She was on Trilling Two, finishing endocrine consult rounds.

"I got Andy to cover your service," she explained.

"That's great. Look, you have to find Griffin Garrett and stay with him, don't let him out of your sight until I get there."

"You're kidding."

"No."

"What's going on?"

"I'll explain everything later. He's on the list."

"No! I can't believe it."

"I'll be there as soon as I can." I hung up, though she was still talking as I replaced the receiver. Too late. Next I called the taxi company for my ride back to the train station. Fifteen minutes later, with no cab in sight, a laundry truck arrived to make a pick-up and delivery at Vista View. I gave the driver twenty bucks to drop me at Union Station. By the skin of my teeth I made the 3:37 to Grand Central. Mercifully there were no major delays, and two subway rides later I was dashing through the main entrance of the Medical Center.

CHAPTER THIRTEEN

I stopped in the doctors' lounge to retrieve my white coat, even though I wasn't headed for the floors. In the Medical Center I always feel more protected wearing my white coat, so I squelch my indignation at the unjustness of hospital uniforms. Doctors are given an extra coat to put on, nice and crisp with pockets and long sleeves, and patients are stripped bare and thrown a tissue of formless cloth. Nonetheless, I was suiting up for Griffin Garrett's reception. I guess I felt like I needed protection.

The party was just getting started when I reached the Treemont conference room on the second floor of the South Building, the usual venue for such events. A projector was set up, no doubt for a slide show to recount the glory days of the neurosurgery department under Dr. Garrett's leadership. The projectionist was fiddling with the machine as early guests arrived and milled around a table spread with hors d'oeuvres, a more deluxe assortment than that usually enjoyed at a Lafayette reception. The department of neurosurgery must have sprung for it. Dr. Garrett stood at one end of the table, dressed in a dark suit and tie, conversing with two women I didn't recognize. From a distance, and speaking to women who probably weren't doctors or nurses, he appeared neither supercilious nor inappropriate. I wondered if he was lit. The women seemed to be enjoying themselves. Garrett, though in his late seventies, was still tall and fit and undeniably good looking with his perfect straight nose and angular jaw. But his long, narrow eyes, the color of cement, gave me the creeps. What could Aunt Selma have been thinking? It was too grotesque to contemplate.

Standing unobtrusively behind him was Jessica. Before I relieved her of her charge, I had one other task to complete. I looked around for Roberta Garrett, but she appeared to be missing. She couldn't have been far, I reasoned, so I headed for her office.

It was a quick trip to the pathology catacombs in the South Building sub-basement. Just outside the Treemont conference room was the staircase that terminated in the back of the main lobby, and from there I traversed the atrium to the rear stairwell that led to the basement and sub-basement. I emerged at the end of an unmarked corridor, and as usual had to hunt up and down the yellow labyrinthine tunnels until I found the right office. The door was open, and Roberta Garrett was sitting at her desk speaking into a hand-held dictation machine. She stopped in mid-sentence and clicked it off when she saw me standing in her doorway. "May I help you?" she asked in an unhelpful tone.

"I'm Nora Sternberg," I said. I had never previously had a conversation with her.

"I know who you are."

"Good. I have to talk to you about something urgent." Although the corridor was completely lifeless, there were two open offices across from hers, so I closed her door.

"I can't imagine what this is about, but it's really not a good time," she said, incredulous and annoyed. I couldn't help notice that her desk was in perfect harmony with her person, each compact and neatly arranged. She wasn't actually good looking, in fact she had deep circles under her eyes and her mouth was too thin. She wore a pair of shiny silver bead earrings that made the whole effect even more severe. The thing that was fascinating about her, I could see immediately, was the way she was looking at me. It struck me as viscerally antagonistic, but I could imagine that to another viewer, for example, a man, her expression might appear seductive.

"Is this a clinical matter?" she asked.

"No, it's personal," I said.

She stood up, but remained behind her desk. "Can you please be quick? I'm due at my father's reception."

"Right, your father. Okay. Well, I'll be as quick as I can." We faced each other across her desk, and I was surprised, for some reason, to realize that we were about the same size. I think I had been under the impression that I was taller. "There are two related events that occurred thirty-five years apart. The first is an operation that went awry. A neurosurgeon operated on a woman with a brain tumor but got his patients mixed up and performed a lobotomy instead, leaving the tumor in." I was ad-libbing a little, on the assumption that if she knew about the operation she probably wouldn't know the details. "He made a big mistake, never acknowledged, in fact, denied—though there are people alive today who know about it."

I paused for air and struggled not to blink. She continued to stare at me impassively, except for a slight twitching of her lips. "The second case," I continued, "is current. A doctor has an affair with another doctor's husband. The husband decides to jilt her, the girlfriend, that is. So, motivated by jealousy or vengeance, or maybe both, she tries to get the wife in trouble. She knows—everyone knows—that the wife has a history of sciatica, so she steals narcotics from several floors in the hospital and plants them on the wife. She even disguises herself to cast suspicion on the nurses."

"You're out of your mind," she interrupted me.

I ignored her. "Now the interesting part is how these stories are related. I won't burden you with the details, but speaking hypothetically, if the narcotics were discreetly relocated where they belong, perhaps no one aware of the neurosurgeon's mistake and cover-up would feel impelled to announce it publicly, right at the moment of his glorification."

She took her time answering, and when she did, she spoke in a voice that could have been measured in degrees Kelvin. "What if I said I have no idea what you're talking about, and I think you're harassing me?"

"Go ahead," I said. "I'll see you at your father's reception. I have nothing to lose by this, you know," and I started to turn towards the door, holding my breath.

There was no back-up plan, and I don't know what I would

have done if she hadn't taken the bait. Finally, just before my fingers reached the doorknob, she said, "All right."

I swiveled around. "Do you know where Dr. Byrd's office is?" I asked.

"No. Yes."

"And you must have gotten the letter, so you know what to do."

"Did you write that letter?"

"Of course not," I sniffed.

"It's pathetic."

"Shut up."

She stared at me with immeasurable hostility.

"Give me the letter," I said.

She didn't answer for a minute, and then said haughtily, "I don't have it."

"Give me the letter, or the deal's off."

"I threw it out," she said.

"Believe me, it will not pain me in the least to expose your father."

She flinched as I said it. "You're disgusting."

I held out my hand and she unlocked a drawer in her desk, pulled out her pocketbook, unzipped one of its compartments, and handed me a folded piece of paper. I recognized Celine's handwriting immediately but scanned it to make sure.

"She put you up to this," Roberta Garrett snarled at me.

"No, dummy, she doesn't know it's you."

She looked absolutely stunned. "Wh-what did you call me?"

"I really didn't mean to call you anything," I said, stating the truth. This time I grasped the doorknob, opened the door and walked out, letting it shut behind me.

I stood with my back against the cinderblock wall and closed my eyes, waiting for my heart to stop pounding, which seemed to take forever. No sound came from Roberta Garrett's office. I realized I was still holding Celine's letter in my hand and shoved it in my pocket. Then I headed up the corridor the way I had come. When I passed a dumpster parked against the wall, I tore up the letter and dropped the pieces in it.

The noise from the party was now outside of the Treemont conference room. A sizeable crowd had gathered, and I had to maneuver my way into the room and over to Griffin Garrett. He was standing in more or less the same place as before, surrounded by acolytes and Medical Center brass. Mr. Irnings was shaking Garrett's hand and pounding him on the back as Bob Schift placidly looked on. In my peripheral vision I saw Jessica still at her post. I waited for an opening to speak to Garrett, edging closer whenever someone in his vicinity drifted away. Eventually there came a moment when he was unengaged, and I seized it.

"Dr. Garrett, I know this is an awkward time," I said, "but I need to speak to you urgently, in private."

He looked at me as if I were some kind of interesting biopsy specimen. "Do I know you?" he asked, not unpleasantly.

"I'm Dr. Nora Sternberg," I said. He continued to smile blandly. "I'm an internist at PCIMC, and I was a medical student and resident here." I was aware that I was speaking too excitedly.

"Well, Dr. Sternberg, this is indeed an inconvenient time for me to speak with you privately." His tone was arch.

"It's absolutely urgent," I persisted.

His smile vanished, and he said sharply, "Are you nuts?"

I shook my head and said, speaking in a low voice but with exaggerated enunciation so he couldn't fail to understand, "It has to do with my great-aunt, Selma Sternberg. I believe you knew her well."

It was interesting to watch the change that came over him. His imperious expression gave way to alarm, which was in turn replaced by the same ferocious hostility I had observed in his daughter. I suppose he thought I was going to blackmail him, not knowing I had a one-a-day rule. Bill Shell was approaching him, but Garrett excused himself and headed for the door. I followed him down the staircase to the lobby and across the atrium to the doctors' lounge. He opened the door with his ID badge, we both entered, and I made a quick sweep to make sure we were alone.

"I'm very sorry to pull you away from your reception, Dr. Garrett, but I have to warn you that you're in great danger," I said.

"Danger from what?" he sneered.

"Someone, I don't know who, is murdering all the nurses and doctors who were in the operating room when you resected the wrong part of that woman's brain. You must remember." He staggered forward, and I stepped back instinctively, but continued, "Whoever it is killed my Aunt Selma, a nurse named Margaret Eichling, Sheldon

Pomerantz, and Harris Townsend. Obviously, you must be a target, too."

"I don't know what you're talking about," he said, "Do you take drugs?"

"Don't you get it?" I pleaded in exasperation. "Someone is going to try to kill you!"

He stood next to the round table in the center of the room gripping the back of a chair with one hand and slowly stroking his forehead and temples with the palm of the other. I stood in front of him, my back to the door. I had expected him to ask me how I knew what I knew. Wasn't he interested? Instead his hand dropped to his side, and he closed his eyes and compressed his mouth into a taut, wrinkled line. He seemed to be entering a trance. I stared at him with no idea what to do. Behind him the television was tuned to CNN, and I must have had an out-of-body experience, because I suddenly saw the screen up close, the anchorwoman announcing, "Smart Weapons when we return." The room was stifling. I have to get out of here now, I thought, just as he seemed to wake up and took a step toward me.

I jumped back, and he said, "Please forgive me, I'm utterly shocked. I'm very grateful to you." I nodded my head, not knowing what to say. "It's warm in here, isn't it?" he asked in a soft, almost kindly voice that I had never heard before, as he removed his suit jacket and placed it neatly on the back of the chair next to him. "What you've said is too horrible to contemplate." He unknotted his necktie. "Have you told anyone else about it?"

I shook my head. "I have to go now, Dr. Garrett." My mouth was so dry I could barely force the words out.

"Of course," he said. "Thank you so much for warning me." I turned and bounded toward the door and had almost made it when he grabbed my arm and pulled me back. "We're not done yet," he said. He was holding his loose tie in his hand, and just as I realized what would happen next he slipped it around my neck and started to strangle me.

I sank down on my knees but he pulled me up. I dug my fingers under the edges of the tie at my throat, trying to pry it loose as he tightened it. He was hunched over me and I kicked him in the shins, but I couldn't knock him over. He howled in pain and cursed, still pulling the ends of the tie. I was doubled over, flailing my arms, unable to breathe, trying to reach his face and stick my fingers in his eyes. I didn't hear the door open, but I felt the tie slacken. Slowly twisting around, I looked up to see Michael Carter holding a gun.

CHAPTER FOURTEEN

"Haven't you killed enough people already, Griffin?" Carter asked in an eerily conversational tone.

Garrett released his hold, and I fell forward onto my knees, sputtering and choking.

"What the hell are *you* doing?" Garrett asked.

I would have wondered the same thing if I could have thought of anything except escaping for my life. I started to crawl away from Garrett, heaving myself across the floor toward the opposite wall. The distance couldn't have been more than four feet, but it seemed to widen as I advanced. An armchair was positioned against the wall, undulating in front of me. I just had to reach it and I could use it to pull myself upright. Carter lurched forward, toward Garrett, and I automatically snapped my head up to look at him. If my neck isn't broken already that ought to do it, I thought, but apparently I could still move my extremities. Carter watched me but kept the gun pointed at Garrett.

"You don't know who I am, do you, Griffin?" Carter said. "You knew my mother, Imogene Carter."

Garrett stared at him and whispered, "Carter." Then he gestured at me and said, "She knows you killed all of them." I was still on the floor, almost at the edge of the chair.

"If you just get rid of her, I'll never tell anyone. I'll give you anything you want. What is it you want?" Garrett was standing with his back to the round table, facing Carter. His shirttails were hanging out of his pants, and the shirt was stained with sweat. Streaks of dirt ran down each of his pantlegs, left by my shoes. His twisted necktie lay discarded on the floor.

I grasped the arm of the chair, hoisted myself up and slumped against the wall, leaning on the chair, so that I could watch them both. Carter wasn't quite as tall as Garrett, but he was equally fit and more than thirty years younger. Dressed in a dark suit, he looked cool and almost relaxed, except for his right hand which was clamped on a gun. "I didn't kill them all, Griffin, you know that," he said in a voice that was oddly soothing. "You got to Harris Townsend first."

"*What?*" I gasped, coughing up a bolus of bloody sputum. A sickening taste of metal gushed into my mouth, as if I had filled it with coins. Did they put iron in coins? Were nickels still made out of nickel, and pennies out of copper? I was becoming disorganized. Can't lose consciousness now, I thought, and I gripped the chair arm and hung my head down to maximize cerebral blood flow. One or the other of them would surely kill me.

Carter kept his eyes on Garrett. "Were you copying me, or do great minds think alike?" he sneered.

Garrett didn't say anything. The room was quiet except for the soft buzz of the refrigerator in the alcove and Garrett's heavy breathing. He had killed Harris Townsend. I was stunned.

Garrett took a step forward, toward Carter, and said, "I don't know what you're talking about."

"Stay where you are!" Carter exploded, and Garrett froze.

"That's better, Griffin." His tone was suave again. "Well, I'm talking about how you killed your old colleague Harris Townsend. Was he blackmailing you? Why didn't you kill him sooner?"

Garrett stared at him savagely.

"Because he only started blackmailing him recently," I wheezed, which was the best I could do, then broke into another spasm of coughing.

Garrett shot me a poisonous look and said to Carter, "I had nothing to do with Harris Townsend's death. Just get rid of her. She's the problem. We can work something out."

"No, Griffin," Carter said, as if correcting a child. "You're the problem. You botched my mother's surgery, then you denied it. Everyone except you makes mistakes, right? When my father sued you, he was labeled a crackpot and humiliated."

"Your mother's death was due to a post-operative complication—," Garrett began, but Carter cut him off.

"My mother's death was due to the neurosurgeon thinking he was operating on a different patient and performing a lobotomy instead of removing a brain tumor!" he shouted. I was still holding onto the armchair, propped up against the wall, almost doubled over. His ranting won't save me, I thought. A hallway and thick door separated us from the outside corridor, and the noise from the party upstairs would drown out his voice.

"Your mother died from a stroke, not her brain tumor," Garrett said contemptuously.

Carter opened his mouth and closed it. He stood very still and spoke softly. "I wanted to see you die in a hospital bed like my mother did, but when these—" he grimaced, "festivities were announced," he pointed the gun momentarily at the ceiling, "and your big award, I knew I couldn't wait. I'd be damned if I sat back while you were enshrined in the Lafayette pantheon." He spat out the last two words like rancid food. "So here's what we're going to do." He reached for one of the chairs at the round table, pulled it out, and gestured to Garrett with the gun. "Have a seat, Griffin."

Garrett stayed where he was, standing in front of the table and facing Carter. "Don't be so formal, Griffin, I'm asking you to sit down," Carter said, advancing on Garrett and jabbing the gun into his neck. Garrett side-stepped to the chair, keeping his eyes on Carter, and sat down.

"Thank you, Griffin," Carter continued with mock politeness. He stood next to Garrett, alongside the table, and threw me a glance, I guess to make sure I hadn't moved. Then he produced a pair of black gloves from the inside breast pocket of his jacket and started putting them on using sterile technique, holding the gun in the alternate hand. Once that was done, he reached inside his jacket again and took out a small pad of paper and a pen. He laid these on the table in front of Garrett. "I'll dictate," he said, and positioned the gun against Garrett's right temple.

"On May 21, 1959," Carter began, but Garrett sat rigid in the chair and didn't lift the pen.

"Pick up the pen," Carter growled.

Garrett sat still. Carter pushed the gun into his skin, and Garrett, without moving his head, looked up at Carter and sneered, "I won't do it."

"You'll do it, you bastard!" Carter bellowed. He grabbed Garrett by the collar, lifted him from the chair, and slammed him to the floor. It all happened in an instant. Garrett's head hit the ground with a loud thud, and immediately a pool of blood began to spread around his skull. He's dead from head trauma, I thought. It was unbelievable. Garrett, the face of neurosurgery at Lafayette for so many years, just had his head smashed to death in front of me.

Carter squatted down and felt for the carotid pulse. Then he stood up and kicked Garrett's body onto its back.

I started moving toward the door, inching along the wall so Carter wouldn't see me out of the corner of his eye. Despite the boisterous party upstairs, I was breathing so loudly I was sure he would hear me. His back was still turned as I stretched out my hand for the doorknob. My fingers touched it just as he reeled around and saw me. My palms were so slippery from sweat I didn't think I could turn the knob. Carter grabbed the gun from the table where he had dropped it. I heaved the door open a crack, but there was a deafening explosion, and I was gone.

CHAPTER FIFTEEN

I awoke in a hospital bed. A nurse with a serious expression was doing something to an IV bag at my side. She glanced at me and said, "Hello there."

"Hello there," I answered.

"I'm Gwen, your nurse."

"Thank you. I'm—" I was interrupted by a head-splitting clanging. I tried to shout, "I'm Nora," but my throat was sore. She nodded as she retrieved a small colorless pouch from her pocket, hung it next to the IV bag and piggy-backed the tubing.

I pointed at the bags and she yelled, "Ancef," a popular antibiotic, especially among surgeons.

Ancef, I thought. How curious.

Behind her, the curtain that bisected the room was pulled back, exposing a second bed, empty, but unmade. Gwen saw me eying the other bed and shouted, "You had a roommate, but they came for her."

I mouthed the word, "Who?" and she hollered, "Miss Dickinson."

I'm glad it wasn't Death that came for me, even though Emily always expected it. Anyway, I was under the impression that Death came unaccompanied. I was oddly aware that I was confused.

The clanging stopped and was immediately followed by a monstrous drilling noise that seemed to be moving closer. "What's happening?" I tried to project.

"They're fixing— " Gwen screamed, and the drilling abruptly stopped. "Oh," she said in a normal voice, and cleared her throat. "They're fixing the ceiling."

She had finished with the IV and was rearranging a pillow under my leg.

"What happened to me?" I asked.

"You've been in surgery," she said.

"I have?" I tried to prop myself up but this involved shifting my left hip, which was extremely painful. "Oh yeah," I said. "I think I remember being in the Recovery Room." Gwen stood at the foot of the bed, scrutinizing the linens. "What was I in surgery for?"

"You had a gun shot wound to the hip," she replied.

"GSW left hip," I mumbled. Then I panicked and sat bolt upright, heedless of the pain. "Where's Dr. Carter?" I asked.

The drilling recommenced at a higher pitch. Gwen said something I couldn't hear. A young woman wearing a hairnet and a tan smock walked into the room carrying a meal tray and set it down on the table by my bed. Gwen shook her head and said something that neither of us could hear. The food service worker smiled and left. Gwen's eyes widened momentarily, then she picked up the tray and carried it outside. I surveyed my situation. The door to the corridor was the only way in or out. There was a window, but I doubted it opened, and in any case, since I had a hip problem I must have been on the orthopedic floor, which was seven stories above the concrete. If Carter found me I was a dead duck.

The room was essentially unadorned. There was a printed sign on the wall facing my bed, titled "Patient's Bill of Rights." I tried to read it but the print was too tiny. An empty bedside table, the long narrow kind that juts across the bed and is impossible to dislodge when you're making rounds and trying to get near the patient, hung over my feet. At the head of the bed stood a square-topped night table with a telephone and a card printed in a swirly font from the ladies' auxiliary. It occurred to me that these might be the last things I ever saw.

I inspected my left hip, and it was bandaged, sure enough. Palpating it here and there I located a spot that was exquisitely tender. I remembered Brad's observation, after he sprained his ankle stepping off the stage while directing *Our Town* in San Diego, that doctors just keep jabbing you, saying "Does this hurt?" until they find the place that really hurts and you scream "Yes!" Except in his personal life, Brad avoided doctors.

Gwen returned, leaned over me and spoke loudly in my ear, "Do you need pain medicine?"

"Where's Dr. Carter?" I asked.

"Oh," she hollered, "I'm sorry, I thought you heard me. The police have him."

The drilling stopped again, as a second young woman in a hairnet and tan smock entered with a tray.

Now Gwen was exasperated. "She's NPO!" she protested, meaning I couldn't eat or drink anything.

"Oh, *sorreeeey*," the new food service person said as she spun out the door.

"Good thing I was standing here," Gwen muttered.

"Not even coffee?" I asked.

"Coffee? You must be kidding," she said. "I have a message for you. Another doctor—wait, I have it in my pocket." She fished a slip of paper out of the front pocket of her uniform. "Here, I have it. Dr. Harvey asked me to page her when you woke up. Would you like me to do that now?"

"Yes, please. Who operated on me?"

"Dr. Pirello."

Pirello was one of the senior orthopedists at the Medical Center.

"Has he been here already?"

She shook her head. "The residents were here. He'll be by after he gets out of the OR."

I thanked her. Reassured that Carter wasn't at large, I relaxed a little and waited for Jessica. She arrived within minutes, breathless, and pulled up a chair by the bedside.

"I already spoke to John Pirello. The surgery went fine," she announced.

"Everybody knows what happened to me except me," I complained.

"Carter shot you."

"Well, I figured that. But all I remember is a big bang, and then I woke up here."

"Wow, you sound just like a patient," Jessica said. " 'I blacked out, and when I woke up I was in the hospital.' "

"So how come he didn't kill me?" I asked.

"He's a terrible shot. He missed the security guard, too. Well, almost. The bullet grazed his arm. It's strange when you consider how good he is with a scalpel."

"Well, you don't throw a scalpel," I said. "It's much easier to aim."

"Yeah, I guess so." She shuddered. "It's all over the hospital that he beat Griffin Garrett to death."

"Not exactly. If I remember it right, he picked him up out of a chair and threw him on the floor. Garrett hit his head. I think he probably died instantly."

"So what was it all about?" she asked eagerly. "No one knows, and everyone's going nuts speculating."

"What's the official Lafayette line?" I wanted to know.

"Oh, that Michael Carter had a psychotic break and went on a homicidal spree in the doctors' lounge," she replied. "But no one, at least not on the staff, is going to believe that was the whole story. People knew Carter. He never acted like a maniac."

"Would you believe it was revenge for his mother's death after an operation Garrett performed on her—more than thirty years ago?" I said.

"I knew it!" she exclaimed, slapping her hand on the arm of the chair.

"You did?" I was astonished. "How could you possibly have known that?"

"Well, not that. I mean, I knew it wasn't random, which is what the hospital is going to maintain. But how is this connected to your aunt? Or is it?"

I proceeded to tell her the whole story, from my epiphanic second trip to New Haven to the scene in the lounge, omitting the identity of Aunt Selma's child and the entire Roberta Garrett chapter.

"Your interview with Mrs. Townsend wasn't wasted," I said. "Townsend must have started blackmailing Garrett because of his wife's gambling debts. I guess he was thinking along the same lines as Carter, that Garrett's pending canonization by Lafayette made the timing favorable."

"Unbelievable," Jessica said. "It's so sordid. That Garrett would operate on the wrong side of Carter's mother's brain and cover it up like that, and Carter would be so scarred that he'd turn out completely twisted. Well, at least we know John Pirello's a straight arrow."

"Well, we think so," I said. "And by the way, wasn't talking to Pirello a violation of my privacy?"

She made a face. "Give me a break," she answered. "Anyway, your cousin Inez insisted I call him."

"Inez?" I asked. "Why did you speak to Inez?"

"Well, you gave your emergency contact as Brad, naturally, but you were sort of hemorrhaging and delirious, and all you could say was that he was in Bergen, and I remembered that he was in Norway, so I tracked him down for the orthopods. Pretty good, huh?"

I nodded, impressed.

"He asked me to call your cousin in Hoboken, so I tracked her down, too, which wasn't easy because he couldn't remember her last name—"

"Diamond."

"Right, but he couldn't remember that. He just knew it was some kind of jewel, and he said her husband's name was Charles, but that's her son. Is he bad with names, or something?"

"Terrible," I said.

"Isn't that bad in the theater business?"

"It's awful."

"Hmm," she said. "It turns out there's a C. Ruby in Hoboken, and several Sapphires, but finally I found your cousin. She was terrified that something horrible was going to happen to you in the OR. I didn't know how much she knew—"

"She knew a lot," I said.

"Well, I didn't know. So I told her not to worry, that you would be fine, but I guess she didn't believe me. She wanted me to contact Pirello and have him call her immediately, and if I wouldn't do that she was going to call the police, though to do what I don't know."

"She was afraid I'd go the way of Aunt Selma," I said sadly. "Did she speak to Pirello?"

"No, I was finally able to convince her, but I had to actually say the killer had been caught. I expected her to ask me more, but she didn't. Then I ended up talking to Pirello in the ER anyway, and I happened to see him in the coffee shop early this morning."

"You know, I've never seen any of the surgical attendings in the coffee shop in the morning," I reflected.

"Of course not. They hang out in the lounge. But it's off limits now, yellow police tape and everything."

"Wow. That must look impressive."

"It does."

"OK. Now tell me what happened after I was shot. How could security have gotten there so quickly?"

"Because I called them," she said. "I followed you and Garrett downstairs from the reception. You didn't know that, did you?"

"No, I didn't."

"I thought it was better to be careful around Garrett."

"Why? I mean, how did you know that?" I asked.

She shrugged. "I have no idea. It was just an instinct, I guess. As I was following you through the atrium, I saw Michael Carter coming from the South Building elevators toward the lobby. He looked like he was in a hurry, but when he saw you and Garrett—"

"I didn't see him," I interrupted.

"I know, you were too far ahead of him. But he saw you, all right. He came to a complete stop and stood there like a statue, watching you and Garrett go into the Lounge. Then he turned 180 degrees and walked back to the elevators."

"What did you think he was doing?"

"I had no idea, but it looked fishy, so I thought I'd better hang around. I waited in the hall by the back of the atrium. Then when I saw Carter coming, making a beeline to the lounge, I pretended to talk on the house phone, you know, the one on the wall across from the door to the lounge. Although he was so preoccupied, I doubt he even saw me."

"He was improvising at that point," I mused. "He must have gone to get his gun from somewhere."

Jessica continued, "After he went in the lounge I stood by the door but I couldn't hear anything. Then, I don't know, I just got a feeling that the whole situation was dangerous, I mean, really dangerous, so I called security."

"Good call," I said, "your instincts served me well."

"Don't mention it. They busted into the lounge just as he shot you. Then all hell broke loose, as you can imagine. They took you to the ER—"

"I don't remember any of that," I said.

"You were a little shock-y."

"Why did they take me to the ER?"

"Well, they had to stabilize you somewhere. By the way, I have a message from your housestaff team, before I forget," Jessica said. "They wanted me to tell you that the patient you were so concerned about—now I've forgotten her name, I should have written it down— someone you recently saw late at night. Why were you rounding at eleven o'clock at night?"

"It's a long story," I said.

She waited.

"I'm too tired, Jessica."

"All right, well the message is she was transferred to your service after Leon Fabricant realized she was on Medicaid, and she's doing fine. Does that make any sense?"

"Perfect sense," I said, remembering Mildred Downey. The intern with whom I had had my late night rendezvous must have told my team that he had found me in her room.

Jessica looked at the clock over my head and jumped up. "I'm discussing the case at noon conference. I've got to run," she said. She told me she would try to return later in the day, adding "But you should get some sleep."

I was on the brink of dozing off a few minutes after Jessica's departure, when a familiar delegation appeared at the foot of my bed. Uncle Louie, Charlotte, and Inez stood in a row, silently peering at me.

"Hello," I said.

No one answered.

I sat forward, which I was figuring out how to do without exacerbating the pain in my hip too much. "Would you like to sit down?"

Again no one spoke. They hardly seemed to breathe.

"Well, how is everyone?" I tried.

"Why did you get shot at?" Uncle Louie demanded.

"Not 'shot at,' 'shot'," I corrected him.

"Do you think this is funny, Nora?" he said.

I had never seen him this excited.

"We've been so worried about you," Charlotte blurted out.

"Sit down, please," I said, gesturing at the chairs at the foot of the bed. "You can pull up one of those chairs, Inez." I pointed at the pair in the corner, by the other bed.

"Won't someone be using them?" she asked.

"No," I said. "They came for her."

"Who?"

"Miss Dickinson."

"Oh."

Inez brought one of the chairs over, and the three of them, still in their coats, arranged themselves at the foot of the bed.

"Jessica called me," Inez said.

"I know. I spoke with her."

"I didn't know what to think," she continued, looking at me significantly.

"I know you didn't. But you see I'm all right."

"I repeat—" Uncle Louie interjected.

"I was at the wrong place at the wrong time," I said. "Don't you want to take your coats off?"

"We're not staying," Uncle Louie said.

"You're not staying?"

"We just came to see if you're all right," Charlotte said.

"I'm all right."

"Well, I'm going to take my coat off. It's sweltering," Inez said, removing her charcoal-colored pea coat and hanging it on the back of her chair. She also wore a black and gray tartan scarf, which she unwrapped and carefully hung over the coat.

"What do you mean in the wrong place at the wrong time?" Uncle Louie asked.

"Just that. I happened to be in the doctors' lounge when a doctor had some kind of psychotic breakdown." I hated to spout the official propaganda, but it's what I would have told them, anyway. I couldn't help it if the hospital's cover story wasn't any better than mine.

"It's unbelievable," he said. "Does anyone know why?"

"No. He was just psycho."

"One of the doctors?" Uncle Louie asked.

"Yes."

"Where is he now?" Inez asked.

"He was arrested."

"That's good," Charlotte said.

The three of them sat staring at me.

"I'd offer you something to drink but I'm NPO," I said.

"What's that?" Uncle Louie asked.

"From the Latin: *nothing per oral*. It means I can't eat or drink anything."

"That's too bad," Charlotte said.

They didn't stay much longer. Uncle Louie had brought me a copy of the *New York Times*, which I was delighted to accept. Inez said she would call me later. As they were leaving she suddenly turned back toward the bed, leaned over and kissed me on the cheek, startling both of us.

After that, two police detectives arrived to question me. They introduced themselves as Inspector Lamont and Sergeant Trumbull, and they didn't take their coats off either. The inspector appeared to be in his early or mid-fifties, medium height, balding, and not overly concerned with his lipid profile. He was soft-spoken and so low-keyed, I wondered if he was bored. The sergeant was taller, and looked about fifteen years younger with short black hair and a neatly trimmed moustache. I suspected he worked out frequently. Lamont did all the questioning, and I wondered what exactly the other officer's role was. Maybe to poke his boss in the ribs in the event he started to nod off.

I didn't know how much of the story relating to my family history I should reveal, aware that it would be impossible to understand the murders without appreciating what had come before. I told them everything except the detail about Charlotte's birth. The inspector told me Michael Carter had confessed to the murders of Sheldon Pomerantz, Margaret Eichling, Aunt Selma, and Griffin Garrett. He wanted corroboration for Carter's statement that Garrett had killed Harris Townsend, and I said I couldn't provide it but suggested he look into the widow Townsend's gambling debts for a motive.

"You've been very helpful, Doctor," Lamont said without the slightest enthusiasm. He stood up. "I don't think we'll need any more information from you, but just in case, don't go anywhere far." I upturned both palms above my legs. "Yes, well, I realize you're constrained," he added.

I wondered if Carter had also told them about his mother's

operation and the subsequent cover-up. I couldn't think of any reason why he would suppress that information. And if he had told them, how long would it be before it became public knowledge? Would it only come out at his trial, or would the newspapers get it before that?

As if he were reading my mind, Sergeant Trumbull handed me a copy of one of the tabloids, which had been folded under his arm. The headline on the front page blared: *Deadly Doctor Runs Amok*, and in a slightly smaller font: *Victims Other Doctors, One Dead, One Critical.*

"Do I look critical?" I asked in surprise.

"The press exaggerates," Trumbull responded, utterly deadpan.

I handed him back the paper but he said, "You can keep it."

I thanked him, and they filed out of the room.

I was reading the newspaper article, which said nothing about a motive, when Celine arrived. "Thank goodness you're all right, Nora," she said, bypassing the chairs and sitting down on the right side of the bed. You could never accuse Celine of going into psychiatry because of any aversion to microbes or the flesh.

She was skeptical of the official hospital line, that Michael Carter, in the throes of a homicidal psychosis, had gone on a murderous spree in the doctor's lounge, killing Griffin Garrett and injuring me. I told her truthfully that I was too fatigued to provide an alternate explanation, and that Carter had had a vendetta against Garrett and I had gotten in the way. She said she would accept that provisionally and for the time being.

"Listen, Nora," she said, placing her hand on the bed and leaning toward me. "I have some very good news. My desk," she looked at me meaningfully, "is back in order."

"That's great, Celine," I congratulated her.

"Thank you. I have to say I'm pleased with how well my strategy worked. And I don't blame you at all for doubting it."

"I appreciate that," I said, and I did. "All's well that ends well, right?"

She nodded. "And Frank has been so lovely. All of a sudden, it's as if he knew I was going through a terrible experience, and he wants to help."

"Isn't that wonderful?" I said.

At that moment, to our mutual surprise, Frank appeared in the doorway. "Frank!" Celine said, her face flushing deeper than the color of her hair.

If Frank thought that was an unusual reaction he didn't show it. He pulled a chair up to the bedside, sat down on the edge, and said, "Thank God you're all right, Nora." Then he looked at Celine and said, "Hi, Cel," and they held hands. Jesus, I thought, is this how it's going to be now? Of course, he wanted to know what had transpired in the doctor's lounge. I gave him the same response I had given Celine.

"But Griffin Garrett dead!" he said. "It's unbelievable. What did Carter have against him?" I didn't answer, and he continued, "People are speculating that it had to do with hospital politics."

"Well, that's what everyone would think," Celine said.

"Yeah, but I don't believe it. Do you?" he asked her.

So the presumption was that Carter had a vendetta against Garrett and I had chosen an inopportune time to wander into the doctors' lounge. "When you're better we'll take you to Iguana's and you'll tell us everything," he said. Iguana's was a bar located a few blocks north of the hospital. We had all been patrons since medical school.

"You remember that research project I mentioned, on the limbic system?" Frank asked me. He let Celine's hand drop gently, perhaps unconsciously.

"What research project?" she asked.

Frank was being clever, referring to a part of the brain that processes emotion, sexual arousal, and memory. "Yes," I said.

"Did I tell you I decided to drop it?"

"Yes, you did, actually."

"Oh, I didn't recall."

"What are you talking about?" Celine demanded.

"Oh, it was a grant opportunity that came up. I thought I should apply for it, but then I realized I have too many other things going on."

"What would you be doing with the limbic system?" Celine asked

"Well, I'm glad you made that decision," I interrupted.

"Yeah," Frank breathed, "I am, too. Although," he cleared his throat, "Howard thought I should pursue it, and he's disappointed." Howard was the chief of pediatrics, his boss.

"I think it's strange that you didn't tell me about it," Celine said. I wasn't sure if she regarded us suspiciously for a moment.

"Unfortunately, the timing wasn't great," Frank said. "I feel like I left Howard in the lurch."

"He'll survive," I said.

We talked about the twins for a little while, then Celine and Frank stood up to leave. They had tickets for a play, and were going out to dinner first.

"What play?" I asked.

"It's a new play, a musical," Celine said, "called *Once on This Island.*"

"Oh yeah? Who's directing it?" I asked.

"I should have found out for you," she said. "I know you always want to know who the director is."

Frank asked where Brad was, and I told him Bergen, Norway. He thought that was fantastic for Brad, though tough for me. They said good-bye and ran off together happily.

I worked on the *Times* crossword puzzle for the next half hour until Eugene came, bearing gifts. He placed a small green glass vase holding a bouquet of flowers on the night stand, and handed me a bag of cookies from the organic pastry shop and a cup of their excellent cappuccino, scalding hot, the way I preferred it.

"Thanks, Eugene, this is great," I said excitedly as I took the doubled paper cup. "You have no idea how much I've wanted a cup of coffee."

"I can imagine," he said. "Nora?"

"Yes?" I took a sip of cappuccino and laid back against the

propped up pillows to savor it.

"When I heard you had been—shot," he said, leaning forward in the chair at the side of the bed, "I—,"

I took another sip. "Oh, God, Eugene, this is so good. I'm NPO, but who cares. I'm sorry, what were you saying?"

"Oh," he said, sitting back in the chair, "oh, nothing."

"This is the greatest. Thanks."

He smiled.

After Eugene left, I was alone except for the nurse's aides who came in to check my vital signs, and Gwen, and the evening nurse, Alma, who looked at my bandages and hung more IV fluids and antibiotics and pushed morphine. I slept for several hours until John Pirello arrived, took down the dressings to look at the wound, and told me I was doing beautifully, which was reassuring. As soon as he left I fell back asleep.

The phone rang around six o'clock at night. It was Inez and she got straight to the point.

"One of those doctors killed Aunt Selma, right?"

"Yes," I said. "Carter killed her."

"First why, and then how?"

"How is easy," I said. "Probably squirted a lethal dose of potassium into her IV. It would be simple, as long as no one saw him entering or leaving her room. I know he disguised himself as a visitor when he bumped off one of the other nurses on the list. My guess is that Aunt Selma somehow knew about him, she obviously had some suspicions, or maybe she saw him walking though the ER, read his name on his ID badge and put it together. That's why she was so anxious to get away from Lafayette."

"But why didn't she just say so?"

"Well, that's harder to answer. It dredges up a lot of old, terrible stuff that I guarantee will depress you." Of course, she insisted I tell her, so I did.

"So the names on the list were nicknames she gave to everyone who was in the operating room at the time of the woman's surgery. And she was keeping tabs on them, because she knew that the two doctors had died."

"That's right," I said.

"But I don't understand. Why would a urologist be doing brain surgery?"

"Because he wasn't a urologist yet. He must have been a surgical intern at that point. They all have to do some general surgery training first."

I don't know what shocked her more, that I had secretly visited Aunt Bunny, or that Aunt Selma was her grandmother. About the latter revelation she said, "At first it seems like it should change things, but it doesn't."

"I know," I said. "We grew up with all of them around."

"Although I hate to think that creepy doctor was my biological grandfather."

"So don't think about it," I advised, and then realized with chagrin that I was echoing Uncle Louie. "You're nothing like him. You're true-blue Sternberg."

"Thanks, I think. Well, at least it explains the brooch."

"Now you can even wear it," I said.

227

"What should I say to my mother?" she asked, and of course, I had no idea. "Well, I'll have to talk it over with Peter. We'll see."

We hung up, and I slept a few more hours, until I was awakened by a hand touching my face. All I could see was his silhouette against the light from the hallway.

"Brad?" I mumbled.

"So," he said. "Whodunit?"